9

THE NEW WINDMILL SERIES
General Editors: Anne and Ian Serraillier

88

THE WAY OF DANGER

and

THE GORGON'S HEAD

The ancient Greek legends of Perseus (*The Gorgon's Head*) and Theseus, the young giant-and-monster-killer (*The Way of Danger*), are two of the world's great heroic stories. With the help of spirited illustrations by William Stobbs, Ian Serraillier has brought them to life again in contemporary language. His simple, fluent and dramatic style will appeal to young readers who appreciate tales of adventure, while older readers, deprived of the literature of a classical education, will find much that is enjoyable and exciting.

Ian Serraillier

THE WAY OF DANGER

and

THE GORGON'S HEAD

Illustrated by
WILLIAM STOBBS

HEINEMANN EDUCATIONAL BOOKS
LONDON

Heinemann Educational Books Ltd

LONDON EDINBURGH MELBOURNE AUCKLAND TORONTO
SINGAPORE HONG KONG KUALA LUMPUR
IBADAN NAIROBI JOHANNESBURG
LUSAKA NEW DELHI

ISBN 0 435 12088 3

Published by Heinemann Educational Books Ltd
48 Charles Street, London W1X 8AH

Printed in Great Britain by
Morrison & Gibb Ltd, London and Edinburgh

To

ANDREW

and

CHRISTINE ANNE

Acknowledgements

The author is grateful for the valuable help and guidance he has received from the following books:

Leonard Cottrell: THE BULL OF MINOS (*Pan Books*)
Trans. Sir J. G. Frazer: APOLLODORUS (*Heinemann*)
Robert Graves: THE GREEK MYTHS (*Penguin Books*)
C. Kerenyi: THE GODS OF THE GREEKS (*Penguin Books*)
C. Kerenyi: THE HEROES OF THE GREEKS
(*Thames and Hudson*)
Ovid, trans. F. J. Miller: METAMORPHOSES (*Heinemann*)
Plutarch, trans. Bernadotte Perrin: PLUTARCH'S LIVES
(*Heinemann*)
M. Rostovtzeff: A HISTORY OF THE ANCIENT WORLD
(*Oxford University Press*)
J. C. Stobart: THE GLORY THAT WAS GREECE
(*Sidgwick and Jackson*)
Rex Warner: MEN AND GODS (*MacGibbon and Kee*)
Trans. J. M. Edmonds: LYRA GRAECA (*Heinemann*)

THE WAY OF DANGER

The Story of Theseus

Contents

1 THE SECRET OF THE ROCK

AITHRA said to her son on his sixteenth birthday, 'Go into the field, Theseus, and lift the rock at the foot of the olive-tree and bring me what lies underneath.'

Obediently he ran to the rock and tore away the smothering weeds and ivy and tried to lift it. Soon he came back to his mother all hot and breathless and said, 'It is too heavy for me, mother. Why do you ask me to lift it?'

'It was your father's wish,' said Aithra.

'What do I care for his wishes?' said Theseus. 'I have never seen him. I have never heard his name, for no one speaks of him here. All I know of my family is that you are a princess, the daughter of Pittheus, King of Troezen, where we live. He told me once that I had in my veins the blood of Poseidon, the sea-god whom our people worship. Is he my father?'

'You are descended from the sea-god, but he is not your father.'

'Then who is my father?'

'When you can lift the stone I will tell you about him and your own destiny. Be patient till then.'

And Aithra, who had been named after the cloudless sky, calmed his passionate spirit, for the boy had none of his mother's serenity. Yet he was brave and self-reliant. Once, when he was only seven, the great Heracles had dined at the palace. He had taken off the lion-skin he wore and thrown it on to a stool. When the palace children came in, they thought it was a real lion and ran away screaming. Theseus ran away with them, but not because he was afraid. He had gone to fetch an axe from the wood-pile to kill the lion. As well as courage he had ambition and much wisdom for his years. Now he saw that if he was to lift the rock and know his destiny he must also be strong. So he spent his days wrestling and boxing, riding and racing, taming horses, hunting the bull and the wild boar, and chasing the deer over the hills, till he was the strongest youth in the land.

When a full year had passed, he was ready to test his strength again, but he could not shift the stone then, nor the year after. Yet all this time he was gaining in strength and skill and also learning a measure of patience. Meanwhile his mother taught him not to squander his powers, but to set his mind to all that was brave and useful and true.

On his nineteenth birthday she sent him once more to lift the rock. Putting his arms round it, he took a deep breath and heaved with all his might. He tried a second time and a third without success. Then he put his shoulder to it and pushed hard—and felt it move.

'Next time I shall succeed,' he said, 'even if my heart bursts inside me.'

Again he put his shoulder to the rock and eased it up and up an inch at a time, and then with a great surge of energy and a sudden twist rolled it over. On the ground lay a pair of sandals and a bronze sword with an ivory hilt. There was a small hollow at the base of the rock just large enough to hold them.

He picked them up and ran to find his mother.

Off Troezen there is a small island so near the shore that you can wade barefoot to it. The temple of Athene stood here, and Aithra liked to sit on the steps and look out over the bay to the purple mountains of Aegina and the Attic shore beyond. She had finished her prayers and was sitting here when Theseus came splashing through the water, shouting that he had lifted the rock. She ran to meet him, and when she saw what was in his hands she smothered him with kisses.

While he tried on the sandals, she was trembling. They fitted so well that they might have been made for him. Then she took the sword from him and showed him the figure carved on the ivory hilt—a serpent twined round an olive.

'This is the sign of Kecrops, the heroic founder of Athens, who was half man, half serpent. You are descended from him,' she told him. 'Some weeks before you were born your father hid the sword and the sandals under the rock. He told me that, if you were a boy, as soon as you reached manhood and could move the rock, I was to send you to him. He said you were to take the sword and the sandals with you.'

'What is my father's name?' said Theseus.

'Aegeus.'

'And where does he live?'

Aithra pointed across the bay. 'You see the island of Aegina,' she said. 'Beyond it lies Athens, the noblest city in Greece. The soil is not hard and barren as it is here, but rich in crops. Your father is King of Athens, and you are his son and heir to his throne.'

Theseus was silent for a minute.

Then his mother said, 'The time has come for you to leave me. Go in secret and tell no one of your journey, for the fifty sons of Pallas have been plotting to steal his throne. If they knew you were his son, they would kill you.'

'And may I not take you with me, mother?' said Theseus.

Aithra sighed and hid her eyes from him. 'Your father has asked for you alone, not for me. I would give all I have to go with you, but I dare not disobey him. You must find a ship in the morning and sail across the bay.'

'The voyage is too easy,' said Theseus. 'I would rather go by land, round by the Isthmus.'

'No, not that way!' his mother begged. 'You will be killed by robbers and bandits.'

'You are wrong, mother. *I* shall kill *them*—as my uncle Heracles would if he had the chance. I have my father's sword—how can I fail?'

'No traveller who took that road has ever reached Athens alive,' said Aithra.

'Then I will be the first,' said Theseus. 'If I can bring my father proof of my manhood, he will honour me and love me all the more.'

Aithra did not dissuade him. Her son was no longer a boy but a man, and he knew his mind.

2 THE MAN WITH THE IRON CLUB, AND THE PINE-BENDER

In the morning Theseus put on his sandals, his purple tunic, and a soft woollen cloak, and buckled his father's sword to his side. Then he said good-bye to his mother and set off along the coast road to Athens.

7

He had not gone far when the lace of one of his sandals came undone. As he stooped to tie it up, he heard a loud swishing sound close to his head. He looked up and saw a huge bulky fellow standing over him and waving an iron club. This was Periphetes, the man with the iron club. He used to hide among the rocks till a traveller came by and then, if he tried to pass, spring upon him and beat out his brains with the club. If Theseus had not stooped to tie his lace at that very moment, that would have been the end of him, for Periphetes had had plenty of practice and his aim was sure. Theseus had time to jump aside.

'My father gave me this club—my father Hephaistos, the god of fire. He forged it himself in the Black Mountains,' said Periphetes, as he prepared to strike again. 'You will not escape it a second time.'

Again the iron club swished through the air. But Theseus was nimble on his feet and dodged again. Periphetes was slow and clumsy, for he had inherited weak ankles from his father and he limped. His strength was in his arms.

Never before had Periphetes missed twice. His temper crackled like the fire in his father's forge. Then with both hands he whirled the club in the air. But Theseus had drawn his sword and struck at the man's wrist, so the club fell clattering on to the stones.

Theseus snatched it up and, while Periphetes was still stumbling to his feet, quickly finished him off. Then, taking the club with him, he went on his way, leaving the body to the wolves and ravens.

Near Corinth the road turns off to the Isthmus and only a narrow strip of land separates two seas. There is a pinewood here, and on stormy days the wind blows in from the seas, howling and groaning among the branches. This was the sound that Theseus heard as he came to the edge of the wood. Yet no storm was blowing; the sea was blue and quiet and the air was still—where did the noise come from?

Suddenly he stopped still.

'Stranger, help me to bend this tree,' said a deep voice quite near. 'I cannot manage it alone.'

A stone's throw away from Theseus was the tallest man he had ever seen. With his head tucked up among the branches and both arms outstretched, he was tugging at the top of a pine-tree, and rivers of sweat were running down his back. The trunk bent like an archer's bow and the roots began to crack. When he had pulled the top to just within Theseus's reach, he called out, 'Boy, hold on to this tree!'

'Why should I?' said Theseus.

'Because it blocks the road and travellers cannot get by. So does the next one to it. We must uproot them both. Hold on to it while I see to the other.'

'I know that trick,' said Theseus. 'As soon as I catch hold of it you will tie my hands to it. Then you will bend down the other tree and tie my legs to that and let go. I do not wish to be torn to pieces.'

'What makes you think so badly of me?' asked the man, still holding on to the tree.

'I know who you are,' said Theseus. 'You are Sinis, the pine-bender, and that is how you treat everyone who tries to pass. You will not do the same to me.'

'We shall see,' said the man, and he let go of the tree. As it sprang upright, there was a great tearing of leaves and a wrenching and cracking of branches, and all the birds for miles around splashed up in terror from the wood and flew away.

Sinis reached down with his cruel hands to grab at Theseus and wrestle with him, but Theseus dodged and caught him round the knees so that he over-balanced and fell. Then he sprang upon Sinis and they rolled over and over in the mud and the fallen leaves. Sinis tried to crush him with his arms, but Theseus wriggled out of his grasp and leapt up. While Sinis was still lumbering to his feet, Theseus stunned him with his club. He tied his legs to the arched pine-tree and bent down the other tree and tied his arms to that. Then he released both trees at the same time.

So Sinis met the fate he deserved.

And Theseus crossed the Isthmus safely and continued his journey.

3 SKIRON THE BRIGAND, AND THE
FAMOUS BED

THE road which led to the Isthmus was no more than
a rough mule track, and the most dangerous spot was
the bend at the foot of the Crane Mountain. Here the
rocks rose very steeply, and on the left a precipice

plunged down to the sea. Sometimes an avalanche of stones would block the path. Then the traveller had to climb down to the sea and walk along the narrow beach till it ended. After that he had to wade or swim to the place where he could climb up again to the mule track. Luckily for Theseus the path was clear today.

Soon he met a man with wild eyes and wild clothes sitting on a rock, with a bronze bowl full of water beside him. This was Skiron the brigand, and it was he who kept the path clear.

'You may not pass until you have paid me the toll,' said Skiron.

'I have no money,' said Theseus.

'You do not need money. You simply pay me by stooping to wash my feet in this bowl.'

'Is the sea-turtle hungry today, then?' said Theseus.

'What sea-turtle?' said Skiron angrily. 'I don't understand you.'

But he understood very well. As soon as a traveller stooped to wash his feet, he would kick him over the cliff into the sea, where a giant sea-turtle that ate nothing but men was swimming about, waiting to eat him.

'If you look over the cliff, you will see the turtle waiting,' said Theseus.

'And the moment my back is turned, you will push

me over,' said Skiron. 'My wits are not as dim as you think. I tell you, there is no turtle there.'

'You are quite right,' said Theseus. 'Before I climbed up here, I went down to the water and cut off its head with my sword.'

'What!' said Skiron, and he turned and peered over the edge of the cliff.

At once Theseus picked up the bowl, hurled it at his head and knocked him over. Skiron turned six somersaults in the air and hit the water with a loud smack. A huge fountain of white spray rose into the air. When it had subsided, Theseus saw the giant sea-turtle break the surface and plunge down after Skiron for his last meal of human flesh.

Theseus was by now very tired, and, when some hours later he met a young man who offered him a bed for the night, he gladly accepted.

'My master Procrustes is most hospitable,' said the young man, 'and he loves to have a guest under his roof. He is lonely and enjoys hearing tales of foreign parts.'

'I am too tired to tell stories tonight,' said Theseus.

'They will keep till the morning. You shall have something to eat and then go straight to bed. My master's bed is famous—there is no other one like it in the world, for it fits every guest perfectly, no matter

14

how tall or short he is. And you will sleep on it as you never slept before.'

It was almost dark when they came to a river. They were walking along the bank towards the bridge, when suddenly the servant missed his footing and fell in. He shouted for help, but the torrent quickly swept him away.

Theseus dropped his club and ran along the bank downstream till he saw him, thrashing about help-lessly in the foaming water. He jumped in, seized him under the arms, and dragged him ashore.

To judge from his coughing and spluttering, the servant seemed to have swallowed half the river. When he had at last recovered his breath, he aston-ished Theseus by telling him that he must not on any account come to the house with him.

'Why not?' asked Theseus.

'Because you have saved my life, and now I want to save yours. If you lie down on my master's bed, you will never wake up again. If you are too long for it, he will lop off your legs till they are short enough; if you are too short, he will stretch your limbs till they are long enough. He treats all his guests in this way. I am the only one who fitted the bed exactly and he has kept me as his servant ever since. Hurry now and go back the way you came.'

But it was too late for Theseus to go back even if he had wanted to, for a lantern came bobbing towards them in the darkness, and the man who was carrying it was Procrustes. He had heard his servant shouting for help and had come out to see what was the matter.

'I fell into the torrent and this stranger saved me,' the servant explained.

'I shall be glad to reward him with a meal and a good night's rest,' said Procrustes. 'And while he's asleep, we can dry his clothes by the fire.'

'He is in a hurry to get to Corinth,' said the servant.

But Procrustes would take no refusal. He gripped Theseus by the arm and brought him to his house, which was just over the bridge. It was built of rough-hewn stones, and a wild fig-tree grew by the door. Inside a log fire was blazing—there was no other light in the room—and there was a sheep roasting on the spit and jugs of wine on the table.

While the servant prepared the meal, Procrustes and Theseus sat down at the table and sipped the wine. Theseus looked at his host's blue gown and all the gold and silver bracelets on his arms and wondered how many travellers like himself he had robbed and killed. Then he glanced over his shoulder and saw among the shadows the two wooden posts at the foot of the famous bed.

They ate the meal in silence, and when it was over Procrustes said, 'You must be very tired after your journey.' And he showed him the bed.

'It looks too long for me,' said Theseus.

'I will make sure that it fits you,' said Procrustes. 'Just lie down and you'll see.'

'I hate sleeping in wet clothes,' said Theseus. 'I thought you said you would dry them for me.'

'Ah yes, so I did. I will fetch you a tunic,' said Procrustes.

While he was gone from the room to fetch the tunic, Theseus had a word with the servant, who was busy clearing the table. Then he undressed, and when Procrustes brought in the tunic, he put it on and lay down on the bed.

At once Procrustes seized his ankles and fastened them with leather straps to the posts at the foot of the bed. Meanwhile the servant, who knew what to do, tied each wrist with a strap and fastened them—or, rather, pretended to fasten them—to posts at the head of the bed. When Procrustes, on his way to attend to the stretching-gear, was within reach, Theseus grabbed him round the waist with both arms and shouted to the servant to cut the straps on his feet. Next moment they were wrestling together in the firelight, while on the walls and the ceiling their

shadows wrestled like black giants. They knocked
over the table. They hurtled into a wine jar and
smashed it, and the red wine poured over the floor.
Theseus was a natural wrestler, and he soon had Procrustes at his mercy. With the servant's help he laid
him on the bed and tied him down. As Procrustes
fitted the bed exactly, there was no need to saw off his
legs or use the stretching-gear. Instead he cut off his

head with his sword and dragged the body outside for the wolves to devour. Then the servant spread two sheepskins on the floor near the fire, and they lay down and slept. They would not go near the bed.

So it was that Theseus, by his strength and skill and courage, freed the road to Athens of its terrors.

4 THE POISONED CUP

WHEN Theseus reached Athens, the marble temples
and the Royal palace on the hill of the Acropolis were
turning gold in the setting sun. A crowd welcomed
him at the gates and followed him through the streets,
for the servant of Procrustes had run on ahead and
talked of his brave deeds. But Theseus did not linger,
for he was longing to see his father.

The Poisoned Cup

Meanwhile King Aegeus was in the palace at a sacrificial banquet with Medea, his queen. She was a cruel sorceress, dark-eyed, with jewels in her long snaky hair. Many years before, she had killed her two children by a former husband and escaped to Athens in a chariot drawn by dragons. King Aegeus, knowing nothing of her past, had protected her and made her his wife, and she had borne him a son, Medus. Naturally she wanted him to succeed Aegeus as king, and she used her magic powers for this purpose.

When the banquet was over and the guests had gone, she said to Aegeus, 'A young man has just arrived in Athens. His name is Theseus and he is wearing a purple tunic and a soft woollen cloak. I have seen him in my mirror by my magic powers.'

'Why do you tell me this?' said Aegeus.

'Because he is on his way to the palace, sir.'

'Then we must welcome him.'

'He is a criminal and a murderer,' said Medea. 'He has come to claim your throne and will kill anyone who stands in his way.'

'Where is he from, this young man whom you hate so much?'

'From Troezen . . . Why do you tremble, sir, and turn pale? What does Troezen mean to you?'

At this moment the doors opened and a slave came

in. He bowed to King Aegeus and said, 'Sir, a young man named Theseus is here and asks to see you. They say in the city that it was he who cleared the road to Athens of its terrors.'

'Bring him in at once. He is welcome.'

'We will welcome him with *this*!' said Medea, and she pushed before the King a golden cup frothing to the brim with poison. Long ago she had brewed it from the deadly foam that dropped from the jaw of Cerberus, the dog that guarded the Underworld.

Theseus came in and walked boldly up to Aegeus and bowed low. Then he raised his head and looked up for the first time in his life into his father's face. There was such a tumult of feelings in his heart that he could not speak.

Aegeus gazed at him, deep in thought. The youth's noble face and brave bearing touched his heart. It seemed to him that this was no common murderer, but such a one as he would love to call his own son. But because Medea was with him he hid his feelings and said coldly, 'Why have you come to me?'

'Because my father sent me,' said Theseus.

'I have had no message from him,' said Aegeus. 'Who is your father?'

Before Theseus could answer, Medea said, 'My lord, leave these questions till afterwards. The stranger is tired and needs refreshment. This wine will revive him.' And she handed Theseus the golden cup.

The froth had disappeared and the wine was clear and sparkling now. There was about it a fragrance of

roses and a deep restfulness. But Theseus did not drink at once. First he drew his sword and handed it to Aegeus, so that he would recognize the hilt and know his son. Then he raised the cup to his lips.

'Stop!' cried Aegeus, who had seen the serpent on the hilt and now recognized the sword and the sandals, too. And he dashed the cup from his hands, so that the poison spilled on the floor, biting into the marble with a hissing sound.

Then he turned on Medea and with terrible anger cried out, 'This is my son whom you tried to kill. It is you who are the murderer, not he!'

He ordered his guards to arrest her, but he was too late. Muttering her witch songs, she had run to the back of the hall. She wrapped herself in a whirlwind and vanished, and neither her husband nor anyone else ever saw her again.

Still horrified that he had come so near to seeing the murder of his own son, Aegeus embraced him with trembling arms. He asked him about his mother, Aithra, and his grandfather, the King of Troezen. Then he called a meeting of the people in the marketplace and presented Theseus to them. 'This is my son Theseus who will rule over you when I am dead,' he said. He lighted fires on the altars and sacrificed many oxen to the gods. The city was gay with feasting and dancing as nobles and commoners rejoiced together and sang of the glorious deeds of Theseus.

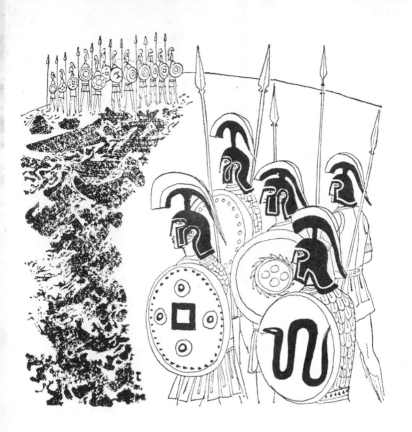

5 THE BULL OF MARATHON

YET all was not well in the kingdom of Athens, and for many years now Aegeus had sat uneasily on his throne. In the hills outside the city lived a savage giant-people, ruled by Pallas and his fifty sons, who declared that Athens belonged to them and that Aegeus had no right to the throne. Now that Theseus had arrived they realized that the throne would never be theirs. So they tried to turn the people of Athens against him, and when this failed they plotted to kill him. They lurked in the shadows and at street corners and hurled spears at him when he passed. Twice they wounded him. Aegeus did his best to keep him shut up in the palace, but Theseus escaped all his precautions and went about the city freely.

There was trouble, too, on the great plain of Marathon, where a fire-breathing bull was ravaging the land. No life was safe, and among the many it had killed was Androgeus, the son of King Minos of Crete. The people of Marathon had appealed in vain to Aegeus to help them, but there was no one in the land brave enough to face so terrible a creature—except Theseus. As soon as he heard of it, he decided to go and kill it, and he insisted on going alone.

Pallas now saw his opportunity. Dividing his sons into two parties, he sent one party to attack Theseus as he was leaving the city gates. The other, which he himself led, he ordered to lie in ambush for Theseus in case he escaped the first party. The spot he chose was the top of a pass between two hills on the road to Marathon. At the last moment a herald betrayed the plans to Theseus, who had no difficulty in disposing of both parties. A detachment of the King's guard attacked the party at the gates and killed them all, while Theseus himself, with fifteen chosen soldiers, marched round the hill and attacked the other party from the rear. Only Pallas and two of his sons escaped, but their position was so hopeless now that they had to go on their knees to Aegeus and sue for peace.

Theseus said good-bye to his fifteen warriors and set off alone for Marathon. The sky was blue and cloudless, but during the afternoon the clouds gathered over the mountains and a great storm broke out, with thunder and lightning and heavy rain. Bowing his head to the rain, he ran until he came to a ruined cottage. He kicked open the door and went inside to shelter till the storm had passed. He was wringing out his cloak when suddenly he realized he was not alone. An old woman was lying on a heap of straw, while the rain splashed down on her through holes in the roof. Her wrinkled face was pale and her eyes closed.

'I am sorry,' said Theseus. 'I did not think that any-one lived here. I was looking for shelter from the storm.'

'I never bar the door to travellers,' said the old woman. 'What is your business, stranger?'

'To slay the bull of Marathon.'

'Then you are welcome indeed,' she said, and she

looked at him intently. 'You may rest here tonight, and in the morning I will tell you what to do.'

Theseus had brought some bread and olives with him, which he tried to share with her, but she seemed too ill to eat. So he made her as comfortable as he could, patching up the leaky roof above her and bringing her water to drink. Then he lay down on the floor and went to sleep.

In the morning when he woke she was already up. She had lit a fire in the hearth and was warming goat's milk for him. While he was drinking it, she told him how to deal with the bull. 'When it charges, stand out of the way of its fire and catch it by the horns. Grasp its nostrils with your left hand. It will stop breathing fire and you can force it to the ground.'

She gave him a rope to tie it with, and off he went. He passed through a village and came to the great plain of Marathon, all scorched with fire, and where the smell of burning was strongest he met the bull. Twice it charged him, its hoofs pounding the earth till it trembled like an earthquake. Each time because of the smoke and the fire he could not reach the horns and leapt aside. But the third time he caught hold of them and grasped the nostrils and forced the fierce creature to the ground. As soon as the horns touched the ground it became tame and quiet, and he fastened the rope to its neck and led it away.

As he returned through the village, the people climbed up trees and stood on the rooftops when they

saw the bull. They hailed Theseus as a hero and showered him with leaves and rose petals as he walked through the streets.

'Who is the swiftest runner here?' said Theseus. 'Let him run to Athens to my father King Aegeus and tell him that Theseus is bringing back the bull alive!'

He stopped at the old woman's cottage to give her his joyful news and thank her, but she was lying stiff and cold on the straw and there were people there preparing her for burial. Sadly he gazed at her face, but the look of contentment on it gave him comfort.

'She must be buried with honour,' said Theseus, 'and a shrine built over her grave.'

They burnt down the cottage and buried her where she had lived and where Theseus had sheltered from the storm. Now a shrine marks the place and the country people worship there.

Then Theseus returned in triumph to Athens, dragging the bull through the crowded streets and up the steep hill of the Acropolis till he came to the temple. There he sacrificed it to Athene, goddess of the city, and watched in silence while the flames crackled and the smoke curled up into the sky. Afterwards he was carried shoulder-high to the market-place, where all the people shouted his praises and hailed him as their future king. All day and all night the rejoicing lasted. By noon of the next day they were still singing and dancing, when suddenly, above all the din, a trumpet note rang out, cold and clear and sounding doom.

6 THE SHIP WITH THE BLACK SAIL

IN all the excitement no one had noticed the arrival at
Piraeus, the port of Athens, of a strange ship with
thirty oars and a black sail. A herald had disembarked
and gone straight to the market-place, and it was he
who had sounded the trumpet.

'Men of Athens!' he cried. 'Have you forgotten
your annual tribute to King Minos of Crete?'

The crowd began to pelt him with stones, till

31

Theseus held up his hand and stopped them.

'What tribute do you mean?' he asked.

The herald laughed at him. 'Are you an Athenian and have not heard of this? Each year seven young men and seven girls from your city are sent to my master, King Minos, as payment for the crime . . . Do you tell me you know nothing of that crime?' he scoffed. 'Have you not heard of Androgeus and what happened to him?'

'He was the son of King Minos and came to Athens to wrestle at the games,' said Theseus. 'Then he tried his skill against the bull of Marathon. He was no match for it and was killed.'

'Aegeus killed him—by sending him to certain death,' said the herald.

'Why was his death so certain?'

'Go to Marathon and see for yourself.'

'I have been there already and have killed the bull,' said Theseus. 'What did Aegeus have against Androgeus?'

'He was jealous because Androgeus had won all the prizes at the games. Ask Aegeus himself if you doubt my word.'

Then Theseus hurried off to the palace to ask Aegeus if what the herald had said was true. Aegeus hung his head and did not deny it.

'It is true,' he said, and he told Theseus about the Minotaur, a hideous monster with a bull's head and a man's body. He explained that the wife of King Minos was its mother, but to the King it had been a disgrace and a bitter shame. He could not bear to look at it. So under the palace he had had a labyrinth built, a maze of such confusion that no one could find the way out, and he had shut the Minotaur inside.

'It will eat nothing but human flesh,' he added, 'and I am bound by treaty to send each year seven young men and seven girls to feed it. For ten years I have done this. I have paid dearly for my crime.'

'You have paid far too much,' said Theseus. 'But we can end this cruel custom for ever. I shall go myself as one of the victims and I will kill the Minotaur.'

'You must not go, my son,' said Aegeus, trembling. 'I need you here. You must succeed me when I die.'

'Let me kill this monster and I shall be all the worthier of your throne.'

When Aegeus saw it was useless to try to dissuade him, he gave his consent on one condition. 'The ship that takes you to Crete has a black sail,' he said. 'You must carry a white sail with you, too, and when you return, hoist the white one in its place. Then I shall know you are safe. I shall stand on the Acropolis and watch for you each day.'

'I will not forget,' said Theseus, and he embraced his father and returned to the market-place. It was almost empty, for the crowd had gone to the Law Courts for the drawing of lots. When he reached the Courts he saw the fourteen victims, seven boys and seven girls, standing on the steps, their parents and friends in tears beside them.

Theseus broke through the crowd and went up to them and said, 'Do not despair. I will go with you and kill the Minotaur. None of you will die.'

Then an old man said, 'For ten years I have seen the victims go. Not one of them has returned. What chance have you when all the others have failed?'

'I have killed Sinis the pine-bender and Skiron and Procrustes,' said Theseus. 'Why should the Minotaur defeat me? The gods are on our side. We must not forget them.'

At once he led his companions to the Dolphin Temple, where he offered the god Apollo an olive branch bound with white wool. Then they went to the harbour. The victim's parents came with them, encouraging them on the way with heroic tales—of how Perseus had killed the sea-monster, and how the infant Heracles had strangled the serpents.

In the harbour the ship was already waiting. The helmsman was standing by the steering-oar; the pilot

at the prow and the thirty oarsmen on their benches were impatient to be off. As the victims embarked, their families and friends followed them up the gangplank, pressing on them food for the voyage, embracing them, clinging to them. And when the pilot cast off the hawsers and the ship drew slowly away, they stretched out their hands to them over the water.

7 KING MINOS OF CRETE

Outside the harbour the sailors stepped the mast in its box and fixed it with forestays; then hauled the black sail up to the masthead and unfurled it. The north wind filled it, and the ship sped away over the waves. But the victims, huddled together amidships, were cold and lonely as the sea, and the crying gulls above their heads echoed their misery.

They sailed past the islands of Aegina and Milos, and on the third day out they sighted far off the cliffs of Crete. A ship came out to meet them.

'She has a golden sail painted with royal dolphins,' said the pilot. 'King Minos himself must be on board.'

The sails of both ships were lowered and the oarsmen took over. The Cretan ship drew alongside. King Minos was standing at the prow, splendid in a golden embroidered cloak that streamed behind him in the breeze. He was a great war-lord and a lover of beautiful things, but he was also vain and given to mockery. When the two ships were close enough for the oarsmen to touch hands, he leapt aboard the Greek ship and asked to see the victims. Trembling with fear, they stood up at the prow, with Theseus beside them. At once a quarrel started. When King Minos saw that there were fifteen and not fourteen of them, he said he would keep one of them as his slave. And he picked out Eriboia, the most beautiful of the girls, and touched her pale cheek with his hand as if she were already his slave. She screamed to Theseus to help her.

Theseus leapt up and stood chin to chin with King Minos and said, 'She is no slave but a noble's daughter. If you touch her again I shall throw you into the sea.'

Never before had anyone spoken to King Minos like that.

'Who are you that dare insult me so?' said King Minos, white with anger.

'I am Theseus, son of King Aegeus.'

'I am the war-lord of Cnossus, king of the islands,' said Minos. 'Immortal Zeus, the king of the gods, is my father.' And stretching out his hands to heaven, he called on Zeus to confirm it with a flash of lightning.

At once the whole face of the sky was split with lightning, and there was a great drum-roll of thunder.

'I have the blood of Poseidon, the sea-god, in my veins,' said Theseus. 'He will give me whatever help I need.'

'Then fetch this,' said King Minos. He threw his gold signet ring into the sea, and it sank at once.

Theseus climbed on to the stern rail and dived into the sea, deep down to the watery halls of Poseidon, the sea-god. And a hundred dolphins, rolling and plunging, brought him to the palace of the Nereids, the daughters of Ocean, who were shining with the splendour of fire. Thetis, the loveliest of the sea nymphs, dressed him in a purple robe and gave him a jewelled crown, her wedding gift from the goddess of love. Meanwhile her sisters swam everywhere to find the golden ring. At last they found it in a cranny of rock and, in front of Poseidon the sea-god, they gave it to Theseus. Then he sped towards the sea-roof, a

long trail of bubbles marking his path back to the
ceiling of light. When he broke the surface, the young
men and girls hauled him eagerly aboard. They were
amazed to see him dressed in a robe even more splendid than King Minos's and not even wet. And when
he handed Minos the golden ring, how they shouted
for joy!

As for Minos, he said not a word, but went back to
his ship and returned to harbour.

8 PRINCESS ARIADNE

In those days Cnossus was one of the great cities of the world. The nearby port of Heracleion was crowded with shipping, with trading-boats from Egypt and Asia as well as the King's own fleet. People had come from all over the island to see the Athenian strangers. They stared at them as they disembarked and marched up the road to the palace.

And what a palace it was! It spread right over the hill. The halls and galleries and countless rooms were built of huge blocks of stone, framed in cypress wood cut from the forests inland. The wooden columns tapered downwards and were painted russet with blue capitals. There was a grand staircase four stories high, lit by wells of light and thus protected from the hot summer sun and the freezing winter winds. It was far more splendid than the palace of Aegeus.

As Theseus entered the hall at the foot of the staircase, he was startled to see a huge black bull in front of him. It had gold horns and white nostrils, red-rimmed eyes and a fierce mouth. At once he thought of the Minotaur. He drew his sword and waited for the charge.

'The beast is harmless,' laughed King Minos. 'Sheathe your sword.'

Then Theseus saw it was only a painting on the wall, and he too laughed. Every hall he entered was decorated in a similar way. There were pictures of wrestling, boxing, and bullfighting. One of them showed the bull-leaping sport, which was very popular in Crete. As the bull charged, an acrobat seized it by the horns, somersaulted over its back and bounced to the ground. There were also scenes from nature—of flowers and birds and trees and the wild creatures of the hills and seas; pictures of the snake goddess whom they worshipped, of processions and public ceremonies, with the Court ladies sitting round and chatting gaily.

It was the custom for King Minos to entertain his Athenian guests to dinner; they were not shut in the labyrinth till the following day. The cups and dishes were all of solid gold; and the food was lavish and magnificent. Yet Theseus and his companions did not feel hungry. They were haunted by the thought of what lay in store for them next day.

In the middle of the dinner they were puzzled by a sudden growl of thunder that seemed to come from underneath their feet. King Minos was quick to explain it.

'The Minotaur is hungry tonight,' he said. 'Perhaps he has smelt human flesh and cannot wait till morning.'

Then the floor began to tremble and the foundations of the palace quivered and shook, and the wine slopped on to the tables.

'The Minotaur is trying out his paces,' said the King. 'His temper does not improve with waiting. But why should we cut short our entertainment to please him?'

King Minos clearly enjoyed his guests' dismay. Not so his daughter, Ariadne, who admired Theseus's dignity and calm. She asked about his exploits on the road to Athens and listened entranced while he told her about them. She could not bear to think of the miserable death that awaited him and his companions next morning. So she decided to help him.

After the dinner she took Theseus to the Hall of Distaffs, where she did her weaving. The walls were bright with deep blue dolphins and star-fish and spiky sea-urchins painted against a pale blue ground, all lit with a soft light.

'Tomorrow I must wrestle with death,' said Theseus.

'I can help you win and escape safely,' said Ariadne. 'Daedalus, the master craftsman who built the labyrinth, once told me how to find the way out.'

She went to her spindle and picked up a ball of wool.

'As soon as you are inside the door, tie the loose end of the wool to the lintel,' she said, 'and unwind the ball as you go. Do not let it out of your hand or you will never find the way back. When you meet the Minotaur, seize him by the horn and stab him.'

'But we are allowed no weapons,' said Theseus.

'Take this dagger and hide it in your tunic.' She gave it to him; the hilt was of solid gold and the iron point sharp as a needle.

'Tomorrow I shall owe my life to you,' said Theseus. 'Dearest princess, what can I do for you in return?'

'Make me your wife and take me back to Greece,' said Ariadne, and the tears welled up in her eyes. 'I am lonely and unhappy here. The palace is full of soldiers; the talk is of nothing but wars and fighting. And at night the monster bellows so loudly that I cannot sleep. I beg you to take me away.'

'With all my heart,' said Theseus, much moved by her beauty and goodness. And he took her in his arms and kissed her.

9 THE MINOTAUR

NEXT morning the palace guards locked Theseus and his companions in the labyrinth. The huge iron door shut behind them with a clang that echoed through the dark twisting passages, the numberless corridors. And when the last echo had faded, there was a dreadful stillness.

'You have nothing to fear,' said Theseus. 'I shall keep my promise. Wait here till I return.'

He had hidden Ariadne's dagger under his cloak. And to light him on his way he had the jewelled crown which Thetis had given him. He fastened one end of the ball of wool to the lintel above the door and set off into the darkness. Crouching by the door, his companions watched the splash of light on the walls till he turned a corner and vanished; then they listened in the pitch darkness to the echo of his footsteps fading into the distance.

On and on down the endless corridors went Theseus, hour after hour, unwinding the wool as he walked. The stone walls were ice-cold and slimy; they glistened wet in the light of the jewels. Sometimes he stopped to look for signs of the monster, to listen for its footsteps.

He had come to a place where the corridor branched into three when he suddenly heard the sound of heavy breathing. He put down the ball of wool and gripped the hilt of his dagger. He peered round and turned his head slowly while the jewels on his crown, shining like a torch, floodlit the darkness. The Minotaur was lying in the mouth of the third passage, curled up, asleep; the monstrous bull's head with its golden horns and white nostrils was nodding over a human chest. Roused by the light, it opened its eyes, red-rimmed and bloodshot, and for a whole minute blinked at Theseus. Suddenly it let out so great a bellow that it seemed as if the walls had

crumbled and fallen in. High above in the palace Ariadne heard it as she sat weaving in her room, and the distaff fell from her hand. The trees in the forest trembled and a great wave rolled ashore and rocked the ships in harbour.

Then the creature scrambled upright. It lowered its head and, snorting smoke from its fiery nostrils, charged. There was no room for Theseus to step aside, but he remembered what Ariadne had told him to do. He reached up with his left hand, caught hold of a horn and wrenched the head backwards. With his right hand he plunged the dagger into its neck. The beast groaned and slumped forward on top of him, almost smothering him as they fell. For a long moment they rolled and wrestled on the stony floor. Then the Minotaur's muscles went limp and slack and it never moved again.

Theseus struggled to his feet. He picked up what was left of the ball of wool, and winding it up as he went, groped his way back to the mouth of the labyrinth where his companions were waiting. They cheered when they saw him and kissed his hands.

But he silenced them at once, for they were not out of danger yet. 'We must stay here till nightfall, till the guards are sure we are dead,' he told them. 'Then Ariadne will unlock the door and let us out.'

At last they heard the key grate in the lock and the door creak open. The stars were shining as they tip-toed out into the warm night. He called softly to

48

Ariadne. 'I have killed the Minotaur,' he whispered. He slipped her hand into his and they hurried down to the harbour, with the seven young men and the seven girls behind them.

The ship was waiting. They hoisted sail and cast off their moorings and steered past the sleeping ships. So that King Minos could not pursue them, they scuttled one of the ships in the harbour mouth to block the way out. Then joyfully they made for the open sea.

When Theseus had washed away all trace of the monster's blood, he took Ariadne in his arms and kissed her. With his companions as witnesses, while the wind filled the sail and tugged at the rigging, he made her his wife. And as a pledge that he would love her all his life, he gave her his jewelled crown and set it on her head, where it sparkled in the darkness as brightly as the stars.

10 THE BLACK SAIL

BUT Ariadne never came to Athens with Theseus. The ship had hardly felt the swell of the open sea when a storm blew up. She ran before the wind all night and most of the next day, then put in to the island of Naxos. Leaving the ship at anchor in a quiet bay, Theseus and his companions landed and found shelter in a cave.

That night while they were all asleep the youngest son of Zeus, Dionysus the wine-god, appeared in the cave. His dark locks were wreathed in vine leaves, and a purple cloak hung from his shoulders. When he saw the sleeping Ariadne, he fell in love with her and was determined to make her his wife and to see that Theseus and his companions sailed away without her. At the touch of his hand on their brows he cruelly wiped away altogether their memory of her.

Ariadne slept on late into the morning, and when she woke she was startled to find that she was alone. Where was the ship? The bay was empty, and the black sail was far away on the horizon. Lonely and terrified, she ran along the shore, cutting her feet on the sharp stones, and weeping. In her despair she cried out to the gods, 'What sort of a man did you give me for a husband? I saved his life, and see how he has treated me.'

Suddenly she heard the sound of flutes and drums and tambourines. Dancing girls came running down the path between the cliffs, each wreathed with ivy and carrying a staff with a pine-cone on the end. Next came a chariot drawn by tigers and lynxes; in it was Dionysus, and fauns and satyrs were running behind him. Joyfully he hailed Ariadne and lifted her into the chariot beside him and comforted her. When she saw that he loved her truly, her loneliness and terror vanished and she was happy again. And the marriage procession danced on. Wherever they passed, the sand turned to grass, and in the crevices between the rocks vines began to grow.

Then Dionysus took the jewelled crown from her head and flung it to the sky, where it faded from their sight. No one ever saw it again by day, but at night it turned to fire, and the jewels that in the labyrinth had lighted Theseus on his way became stars. On cloudless nights you can see them still.

Meanwhile the ship sailed on towards Athens. Theseus sat moodily at the prow and would not speak to anyone, except to urge the sailors to press on home. He drove his thirty oarsmen so hard that they had no time to rest or eat. At last they came in sight of the coast of Attica, and his spirits rose. He longed to see his father again and to be welcomed as a hero.

As soon as they landed, Theseus sent a herald to the city to tell his father of his safe return. Meanwhile the exhausted sailors put what was left of their provisions in a common cooking-pot, boiled them up and ate them ravenously. Theseus would not touch any food until he had first given thanks to the gods for his safe return. He built an altar on the seashore and laid on it an olive branch wreathed with wool and hung with

the season's fruits, for it was harvest-time. Then he
made gifts of wine. When he had finished, he saw that
the herald had returned from the city and was hovering on the edge of the crowd, not daring to come
forward. His herald's staff was twined with garlands.

Theseus went up to him and asked him his news.

'Sir, the people of Athens rejoice in your triumph
and greet you with these garlands,' he said as he
placed them on Theseus's shoulders.

'Have you no message from my father?'

'He is dead,' said the herald. 'He took his own life. Each day since you sailed he stood on the Acropolis looking out over the sea, impatient for your return. This morning when he saw the black sail he gave you up for dead and flung himself headlong from the rock.'

Then Theseus remembered his promise to Aegeus to hoist the white sail on his return. At once his gladness turned to grief and bitter self-reproach. He would not be comforted. Next day, in deep mourning, he buried his father in a hero's tomb. He would not wear the garlands which the people gave him, but heaped them into the grave. And so that his father's name should not be forgotten, he named the sea that washes the shores of Greece the 'Aegean'.

11 THE WAR WITH THE AMAZONS

THESEUS now became King of Athens. When he had
recovered from the shock and sorrow of his father's
death, he showed himself a wise and far-sighted ruler.
Until now there had been twelve separate communi-
ties in Attica, each managing its own affairs and sometimes quarrelling and fighting with each other.

Theseus persuaded them to unite and to accept a single Council Hall and Law Court in Athens. This was no easy task, and he had to visit each clan and family in turn. The common people and the slaves were the first to agree, and the nobles and the land-owners followed when he promised to let them share the government. He gave up his own Royal power but remained commander of the army and chief judge. He sent his heralds all over Greece to invite the people to become citizens of Athens. When they flocked into the city, he divided them into three classes: nobles, farmers, and craftsmen. The duty of the nobles was to look after religion, supply magistrates, and teach the laws; the farmers tilled the soil; and the craftsmen—the biggest class of all—included doctors, soothsayers, heralds, sculptors, builders, and shopkeepers. He also minted money, stamping each coin with the image of a bull, and established festivals and games.

The first trouble that the new State of Athens had to meet came from the Amazons. They were a tribe of women warriors who lived on the shores of the Black Sea at the foot of the mountains and spent their lives fighting. They had brazen bows and shields like half moons. Their clothes were made from the skins of wild beasts, and their helmets and armour from the tough hides of Libyan serpents. One winter they galloped their horses westwards over the frozen sea, across Thrace and Macedonia and down into Greece, conquering and laying waste the land. A farmer came running into the city and reported that they had burnt down his barns and granaries; afterwards he had seen them dancing round their camp fires to the music of pipes, rattling their quivers and stamping on the ground. During the following days more and more country people left their fields and farms and flocked to the city for refuge. But the Amazons swept on, and soon they were camping outside the city walls.

Theseus led out his army against them, and his infantry showered them with javelins. The Amazons were led by their queen Hippolyta, who was a head taller than the others and the bravest of them all. Yelling their hideous war-cry and waving their swords, they quickly scattered the Athenian left wing. On the right wing the soldiers in the front ranks were trampled by the fiery hoofs, but the rest stood firm and tried to drag the Amazons from their horses. After three charges they were forced to retreat. As they went they turned round in their saddles and with deadly accuracy shot their arrows at the Athenians. Among the wounded was Hippolyta. Theseus had dragged her from her horse and fought her hand to hand until she was swept to the ground by a runaway horse and stunned. After the battle he found her lying on the ground, pale-cheeked and with her eyes closed. He had already admired her courage and now he admired her beauty, too. He revived her with water and had her taken to the palace.

Now that they had lost their Queen, the Amazons had no heart to continue fighting, so they made a treaty with Theseus and left the country. But Hippolyta stayed behind and became Theseus's wife. She bore him a son named Hippolytus, a noble youth who loved hunting and was also a great charioteer.

Meanwhile reports of Theseus's wisdom and strength and bravery were spreading all over Greece. They reached Pirithous, King of the Lapiths, who lived in the north at the foot of Mount Olympus. He decided to see for himself if they were true. So he marched south with a large army and raided Attica. On the great plain of Marathon, which borders the eastern coast, he found a herd of cattle grazing and drove them away. But when he heard that Theseus and his army were hot on his trail, he did not run away; he turned back to meet them.

Theseus's army, mostly infantry, was ranged along a hill and had the advantage of the slope. The army of Pirithous was twice as big and all his soldiers were

mounted. Undismayed, Theseus rode quietly forward on his white horse with his sword drawn. He
did not stop until he was within hailing distance of
Pirithous. He was going to give the signal for the
charge, but he could not do it. Admiration for his
enemy's noble looks and bearing overcame him. He
could see no trace of fear in the King's eyes, and his
limbs were so strong that they might have been
carved out of the living rock. Pirithous felt the same
about Theseus. Sheathing his sword and spurring his

black horse forward, he rode up to Theseus and clasped him by the hand.

'Noble Theseus,' he said, 'I did wrong to raid your country and steal your cattle. I can wish you nothing but good and will gladly submit to any penalty you like to name.'

'The penalty,' said Theseus, 'is that you swear an oath of everlasting friendship with me. And you must ride with me to Athens, where we shall feast and rejoice together.'

Pirithous swore his oath, and they rode away to Athens, each delighting in the companionship of the other.

12 HELEN

SOON after his return north from Athens, Pirithous married a wife named Hippodamia. Theseus was one of the wedding guests; so were the Centaurs, half men, half horses, who lived on the Lapith borders and were related to the bride. Unfortunately they turned the feast into a drunken brawl, and Theseus, out of loyalty to his friend, became involved in a long feud with them. With the help of Heracles he finally drove them away from their ancient hunting-grounds on Mount Pelion and forced them farther inland. Hippodamia died soon afterwards, and Theseus had hardly returned from the war with the Centaurs when he heard that his own wife, Hippolyta, had died, too.

The days of happiness and triumph for Theseus were now over, and the rest of his life was darkened by sadness and misfortune, for much of which he was himself to blame.

At this time Helen of Troy was only a child of twelve. But she was already so beautiful that Theseus was determined to marry her when she grew up. So he and Pirithous went to Sparta where she lived, seized her while she was dancing in the temple of Artemis and galloped off with her. Aithra, the mother of Theseus, was now living in Athens and they handed Helen over to her and asked her to look after her till she was ready for marriage. Aithra soon grew very fond of Helen and treated her as if she were her own child.

One day, when she was teaching her to weave, she heard a scuffle in the passage outside. The door burst open and in rushed two young men with drawn swords. Aithra stood in front of the child, trying to shield her, but Helen showed no fear of the young men and with a cry of joy ran to greet them. They were her brothers, Castor and Pollux. Castor threw down his sword and hugged her, but Pollux stood facing the door, ready to fight his way out. He had not long to wait before Theseus came in, followed by Pirithous and most of the palace guard.

Pollux lunged at Theseus, who found it easy to ward off the blow and knock the boy's sword from his hand. Pirithous put his foot on Castor's sword before he could touch it. The two boys tried to continue the fight with their fists, but they were quickly overpowered and would have been killed had not Theseus intervened.

'Sir, we are Helen's brothers and have come to claim her back,' said Castor.

'You had no right to seize her,' said Pollux. 'Our cause is just.'

For a minute Theseus was silent. Then he turned to Helen and said, 'Is it true that these men are your brothers?'

'It is true, sir.'

'And you wish to go back home with them?'

'I do, sir.'

'Has my mother Aithra not treated you well?'

'My own mother could not have been kinder,' said Helen.

'Then why do you wish to go?'

'Because you forced me to come against my will. I am a stranger here and I belong to my own family, not to you.'

'When you are older you may be glad to return,' said Theseus.

'I could never grow to love you, sir. You are too stern,' said Helen.

There was a gasp of astonishment, for no one in the

palace had ever been so outspoken to Theseus before. But Theseus only smiled. He admired Helen for her calm bravery and her brothers for their courage.

'You have acted nobly and are free to take her home,' said Theseus.

Helen ran forward and knelt and kissed his hand. But Pirithous was angry and indignant.

'Sir, does it mean nothing to you that these young men have killed two of your guards?' he said hotly. 'Wars have been started for less than this. With your army you could soon bring Sparta to her knees.'

'The gods would not bless our victory,' said Theseus. 'I did wrong to seize Helen, and I cannot fight for an unjust cause.'

And he let the brothers go back in peace to their own home, taking Helen with them.

13 THE KINGDOM OF THE DEAD

SOON afterwards Pirithous was talking to Theseus about women and marriage. 'There is one I know who is more beautiful than Helen could ever be,' he said. 'Her name is Persephone, Queen of the Underworld.'

'Then why not visit the Underworld and demand her as your bride?' said Theseus jokingly.

'That is what I mean to do,' said Pirithous. 'The oracle of Zeus has told me she is the noblest of his daughters.'

Theseus never intended his suggestion to be taken seriously. But he had already promised, in return for his friend's support in fetching Helen, to help him find a bride for himself. Now Pirithous bound him to his oath, and Theseus dared not break it.

The Underworld was the kingdom of the dead, from which only gods and heroes ever returned. A sloping path, shaded by deadly yew-trees, led down to it. The marshy River Styx, whose banks were choked with reeds, flowed along the border, and Charon the ferryman took all the dead over in his boat. But Theseus and Pirithous did not go this way. They chose the back way and entered by a secret cavern deep in the Caucasus Mountains, by the shores of the Black Sea. It was called the Cavern of Hades and was bitterly cold, and so dark that they needed torches. For safety they carried their swords as well. Down and down the long tunnel of gloom they went. Presently they heard the sound of barking. At the end of the tunnel they turned a corner, and the darkness faded into twilight, and suddenly a huge three-headed hound stood in their path. It was Cerberus, the guardian of the gates of hell. Each head had a mane of biting snakes, and snakes instead of hair hung from his back. He could swallow anything with his three mouths. He greeted the dead by wagging his tail like a good sheepdog. But he ate all the living strangers he could catch, for he liked his meat raw. With a savage growl he rushed at the two kings, lashing the air with his barbed tail. But he was chained to a stake, and as the links tautened they both managed to avoid his cruel jaws.

Before them stretched the Underworld, a landscape of grey upon grey, merging into heaviest black. There was no colour or brightness at all. They walked across fields of asphodel, flowers that looked like blossoms of grey mist, over which drifted the ghosts of the dead, bloodless spirits without body or bone. If they ventured too near, the ghosts ran away with a soft twittering and whirring sound. They passed the Elysian fields, which were more beautiful than any fields on earth. The leaves on the trees and hedges were black, and the ground was thick with black hyacinths—a hundred blooms springing from a single root and filling the air with fragrance.

At last they came to the palace of a thousand gates where Hades was King and welcomed the newly dead. The palace was roofless, for there was no sun, rain or wind in the Underworld. The two kings

knocked on the gates, which opened soundlessly. They passed into a court of playing fountains and entered a grove of cypress-trees that grew not far from the palace walls. Here, on ebony thrones, sat King Hades and his Queen Persephone. It was their favourite spot, for there was no wall in front of them and they could look out over half their kingdom and watch the rivers that all the dead must cross when they first arrived.

'What is your errand?' said King Hades.

'I have come in search of a wife,' said Pirithous, who always went straight to the point.

'Then you have come to a strange place, for only the shades live here,' said Hades. 'Can you find no lady on earth to please you?'

'No one to compare in beauty with the lady of my choice.'

'What is her name?' said Hades.

'Persephone,' said Pirithous, and he took from his wallet a narcissus, Persephone's favourite flower, which she loved more than lilies or violets, and he handed it to her.

Her pale hands accepted it, but she did not smile or speak.

'And what does your companion want?' asked Hades, apparently unmoved by this impudent request.

'Nothing, sir, except permission to stand by my friend,' said Theseus.

'Then you will need to be very patient,' said Hades, and Theseus wondered what he meant. 'You must both be tired after your long journey. There are two rocks in my garden. Sit down on them and rest.'

The two friends walked unsuspectingly across the garden to the rocky seats they had been offered.

Theseus was the first to sit down. At once he felt his limbs stiffen. He tried to get up, but he could not, because the rock had become part of his flesh. He cried out to his friend to warn him not to sit down. Pirithous was standing by the rock, irresolute, wondering what to do, when a hundred snakes oozed from a crack in the earth. They hissed and spat at him and drove him against the rock, so that he could not help sitting down. Now he, too, was stuck and unable to move. Then the three winged Furies swooped down on them, lowing like cattle. Their skins were black, their clothes were grey, and they had hissing snakes for hair. As they circled above the two kings, they breathed on them with their foul breath and beat them with brass-studded whips.

Hades watched them, smiling grimly. And beside him Persephone was tearing off one by one the petals from her flower and crushing the green stalk under heel. She did not smile at all.

14 THE RESCUE

So Theseus came to the Underworld, where everything was strange to him. There was no cockcrow to greet the dawn, no singing of birds, no wind to stir the branches of the trees, no sound but the whirring of ghosts and the far-away barking of Cerberus. Fixed to his rocky seat, he watched all the traffic of the

Underworld. He could see in the distance the River Styx, and on its sluggish, poisonous waters old Charon's boat with its cargo of newly dead. He watched them step ashore into the country of dreams and, led by Hermes with his golden rod, drift over the cold waste to Lethe, the river of forgetfulness. And as they crossed they trailed their hands in the stream and sipped its waters. By the time they had reached the other side, they could remember nothing of their lives on earth. They belonged now to the innumerable nation of the dead.

Then King Hades, commander of souls and host to many guests, went out to meet them, driving in his black chariot drawn by black horses with silent hoofs. The spirits of the blessed he sent to the Elysian fields, to live there in happiness for ever, but the damned endured eternal torment for their crimes. Among these was Tantalus, who had been here many years. Tortured by hunger and thirst, he could not reach the fruit that hung from the bough overhead or the water that flowed past his lips. Another was Sisyphus, for ever pushing his rock uphill; whenever it topped the summit, it rolled down again to the plain. Another was Ixion, chained throughout eternity to a burning, whirling wheel. To Pirithous this was the cruellest sight of all, for Ixion was his father. And once

Theseus saw his own father Aegeus wandering pale and listless through the palace courts. He called out to him and stretched out his arms. But Aegeus did not know him; he glanced at him with frightened, empty eyes, and then with a whirring sound drifted on.

Many years passed. Then one day Theseus heard something he had not heard since he left the earth—the sound of human laughter. It was louder than the three barking mouths of Cerberus and could come from nobody but Heracles. He was wearing his lion-skin and carried his sword and club. He was ten feet high and very strong, and the muscles on his arm were like a rippling river. Of all the heroes Theseus admired him most.

'Heracles!' he called. 'I am Theseus, King of Athens. Do you remember me?'

Heracles ran to him and held out both hands in welcome. 'We have not met since we fought the Centaurs together. This is a strange place to find you. Why did you come here?'

Theseus told him the reason.

'A rash venture,' said Heracles, 'and I see that you have suffered for it. But perhaps my own venture is no less rash than yours. The King of Argos has sent me to capture Cerberus. Of the twelve labours he gave me to do, this is the last and by no means the

74

lightest. I had to fight my way in with my sword. When I came to the River Styx, Charon refused to row me across because I had no money. He sneered at me and said, "The dead keep a coin under their tongues to pay their passage. What have you brought?" "A scowl," I said, and I treated him to one of my fiercest. He didn't dare refuse again. But it's a wonder I didn't drown in that ferry of his. It's only sewn together from pieces of bark, and under my weight the rim was level with the water.'

By now Persephone and King Hades had seen him and were coming towards him. Persephone had known Heracles on earth before Hades had made her his queen. She now greeted him like a brother. He told her why he had come to the Underworld and asked if he might take Cerberus back with him.

'I will ask my lord,' said Persephone.

'The hound is yours, Heracles, if you can master him,' said King Hades. 'But you must promise to use no weapon—no club, no sword, no arrows.'

Heracles promised. Then he turned to Persephone and asked her if she could yet forgive his friend Theseus his folly. Persephone agreed at once, for she had always admired Heracles and was willing to please him.

'May he return to the world of men?'

'I will ask my lord,' said Persephone.

'Theseus is fixed to his rock for ever, and not even your strength, Heracles, can move him,' said King Hades. But he added, 'You may try to release him if you wish.'

'I will try anything for a friend,' said Heracles.

He put down his club. Then he took hold of his friend's hands, placed his right foot against the rock and tugged with all his might. Three times he tugged, and at the third time wrenched him free. Stiff-limbed and wincing with pain, Theseus stood up. When Heracles saw that his friend had left some of his skin behind, he called it jokingly the price of his freedom.

He next tried to do the same for Pirithous. The snakes that had twined themselves round the King's legs spat and hissed at him, but he managed to uncoil them and break their backs with his club. But when he seized Pirithous by the hands, King Hades raised his arm and in a terrible voice cried out to him to stop. And to show his displeasure he sent an earthquake that shook his whole kingdom.

Heracles knew better than to persist. He bowed low to King Hades and Persephone and quickly led Theseus away.

So it was that Theseus was rescued, but Pirithous stayed behind to suffer torment for ever.

15 THE FIGHT WITH CERBERUS

THE loss of his friend Pirithous saddened Theseus, but
he could not change the will of the gods. As they
hastened on through the twilight of the Underworld,
Heracles talked to him about his adventures, now and
then pausing to stuff a barley cake in his mouth. He

liked to carry food with him, as his huge energy made him always hungry.

'When Charon landed me from the Styx,' he said, 'the ghosts were so frightened that they ran away from me, squeaking and twittering like bats. But two of them stood firm. The first was the Gorgon Medusa. I drew my sword, but Hermes told me it was useless against her—I could not hurt the air. The other ghost was my old enemy Meleager, dressed in full armour. He smiled and said that I had nothing to fear from the dead, and we were friends at once. But imagine—a ghost in full armour!' and he laughed aloud.

Theseus paused in the Elysian fields to pluck leaves from a black-leaf poplar, and with these he wove a wreath for Heracles and put it round his brows.

They crossed the cold, desolate waste, and at last they reached the far fringe of the Underworld, the mouth of the gloomy tunnel where Cerberus was chained. They spoke in whispers now, for they did not want Cerberus to hear them. They hid behind the rocks, slinking from one to the other and guided by the barks. And suddenly they saw him, lying by his stake. Was the hound asleep? Two heads were resting on his paws, but the third was alert, the sullen eyes suspicious. He saw the strangers and knew at once that they were no spirits to greet with wagging tail. Then all of him awoke and he gave three yelps and charged.

They stood out of his reach and waited till the chain that tethered him pulled him up short and tautened with a clang. He pawed the air, and the tunnel under the mountain echoed and re-echoed to his barking. He went back and charged again, and, as the chain tautened, the stake shuddered in the ground. If it failed to hold, what chance had bare hands against three heads of snarling fangs?

But Heracles was ready and did not flinch. The hound had three heads, which branched from a single throat—and there he saw his chance. At the third charge, at the very moment that the chain checked him, Heracles sprang up at his throat and grappled. He pressed with all his strength and held the snapping fangs clear. The snakes on the three heads writhed and hissed. The brute lashed at him with his barbed tail, but the lion's skin he wore protected him from harm. The tighter his fingers gripped, the feebler grew the lashing. The hound began to choke, slumped and lay still. The only sound was the hissing of the snakes, and it was like the hissing of water on red-hot iron.

Heracles stood back, gasping for breath, his huge chest heaving and panting from the labour like a giant bellows. The sweat ran in rivers down his face and along his arms. A strange thing had happened to the wreath on his head. The outer leaves of the wreath were still black, but the inner leaves were bleached white by his sweat. Since that day the white poplar, whose leaves are white underneath when the wind turns them up, has been sacred to Heracles.

'I have not killed the brute, but I have broken his spirit,' said Heracles. 'He will know who is master when he wakes.'

But when Cerberus recovered, he was not as obedient as Heracles had expected. He soon regained some of his strength and struggled to break free. But Heracles snapped the chain in two and used it as a lead; then urged the hound forward into the mouth of the dark tunnel that led back to the world of men. With his huge strength he half dragged him, half carried him all the way, while Theseus stood ready to club his three snouts if he disobeyed. They moved quickly in the darkness, for the eyes of Cerberus were as bright as the sparks that a blacksmith strikes from iron when the anvil rings to his blows, and they lit the way. At last, high above them, they saw a pin-prick of light. It grew bigger as they struggled towards it. It was the mouth of the secret cavern by which Theseus had entered long ago. And now he was standing there with his friend and rescuer at the foot of the Caucasus Mountains by the shore of the Black Sea. The rocks and overhanging trees, chilled by the icy breath of the Underworld, were white with

frost. The strong sunlight made both men half close their eyes till they got used to it again. But Cerberus had only known twilight and darkness and had never seen the sun before. For him the white glare was blinding, and he bounded painfully away along the bleak shore, with Heracles close on his heels. His three mouths were barking and yelping, the snakes on his mane and back were hissing, and wherever his saliva fell a poisonous plant sprang up.

Theseus watched them till they were out of sight and hearing. He was still grieving for his friend Pirithous and very tired, and he lay down in the mouth of the cave and slept.

16 THE GOLDEN EAGLE

ALL the rest of the day and all night he slept, and in the morning he woke refreshed. Full of hope and happy expectation, he set off on the long road to Athens. He could only walk slowly, for his tortures had greatly weakened him, and it was many weeks before he arrived home.

The first thing he did was to build an altar sacred to Heracles his rescuer. Then he went into the market-place and told the crowd who he was. But they only laughed at him and said that Theseus had been dead for many years. So he showed them his sword and the carving of the serpent on the hilt. Most of them refused to accept this as proof. But there were a few old men who had seen it before and recognized in the creased and worn face before them a faint likeness to their king and hero. He asked after his mother, Aithra, and they told him that she had long ago been carried away to Sparta as a slave and no one knew if she were alive or dead. Next they took him to the palace, where Menestheus was now king. He had seized the throne and by bribery and terror made his position safe, undoing all the good that Theseus had done. Menestheus refused to see him and ordered the palace guard to kill him. But Theseus escaped and went into hiding. Gradually he gathered friends about him, but his attempts to regain the throne failed and all ended in strife and trouble.

In despair he sailed for Crete, where the new King, Deucalion, had promised him refuge. As the ship sailed away from Piraeus, he looked across the water towards Athens and solemnly cursed his people.

A storm blew the ship off her course, and she

drifted at the mercy of wind and wave far up the Aegean Sea to the island of Scyros, where Lycomedes, a close friend of Menestheus, was King. Theseus had inherited an estate on the island, and he now asked Lycomedes if he might settle there in peace. Lycomedes agreed and received him with all the ceremony and honour due to a great hero. He gave a banquet for him, then took him up a mountain to show him the boundaries of his estate. From this climb Lycomedes returned alone. He said that his guest had drunk too much at the banquet and had slipped and fallen to his death. The tale was false. He had treacherously murdered Theseus by pushing him over a precipice.

In due course news of his death reached Athens, but no one mourned him. Six hundred years later, when the Athenians fought the Persians at Marathon, it was said that his spirit in full armour rose from the earth and led them to victory. After the battle the priestess of Delphi gave orders that the bones of Theseus should be brought home to Athens for burial. This was a difficult task, for the people of Scyros were wild and barbarous and refused to say where the grave was. Even when the Athenian admiral Cimon captured the island, they still refused, and Cimon was left to search for it alone.

Suddenly he saw a golden eagle swoop down on to a hilltop and begin to tear up the earth with its talons. He took this as a sign from heaven and ran to fetch a spade. He enlarged the hole which the eagle had made and soon struck the stone coffin of a man of extraordinary size. Inside it he found a skeleton and beside it a bronze lance and a sword. It was the same sword that Theseus had found in his youth under the rock and which he had kept all his life.

Cimon had these precious relics carried to his flagship and he brought them home in triumph to Athens, where they were buried with great honour. A temple was built above the grave and decorated with sculptures and paintings to celebrate the hero's great deeds. It was called the Sanctuary of Theseus and became a refuge for runaway slaves and all who were poor or oppressed, for Theseus had always been their champion.

THE GORGON'S HEAD

The Story of Perseus

Contents

THE WOODEN CHEST

ONCE there were twin princes who had quarrelled since the day they were born. Their names were Acrisius and Proetus, and they had hardly grown to manhood when their father died. Which of them was to succeed him as king? They could not agree, and instead of sharing the kingdom as their father had wished, they fought a great battle. Neither side won, so they divided the kingdom between them. Acrisius ruled in Argos and Proetus ruled in Tiryns, which he fortified with massive walls. The blocks of stone were so huge that a mule team could not move the smallest of them. And the two brothers lived apart in enmity and discontent.

Many years later Acrisius went to the priest of Delphi and said, 'I am not satisfied with my life. I have a daughter and no other child. Why do the gods refuse to give me a son?'

The priest answered, 'Because you have quarrelled with your brother and all your family and will not live in peace.'

'Will I never have a son?'

'Never. But your daughter will bear a son, and he will kill you.'

Acrisius returned to Argos, determined that his daughter, whose name was Danae, should never become a mother. In the court of his palace he had a prison built for her, underground. The walls, the floor and the ceiling were made of bronze, and he shut her inside and set two fierce dogs to guard the entrance. There she lived, buried away in the cold and the darkness, far from the light and warmth of the sun. She saw nobody at all except the nurse who brought her food once a day.

But with the gods all things are possible. One day a shower of golden rain poured through the bronze roof. Danae caught it in her lap, and out of the golden shower stepped Zeus, the king of the gods. The prison became a marriage chamber, and in the course of time Danae became the mother of a son. She called him Perseus.

Some days after Perseus was born, Acrisius was walking in his courtyard when he heard a baby's cry. It seemed to come from the prison below. He seized the nurse and questioned her, but she would not speak. So he hurried down the steps to see for himself. He was so angry and impatient that he had forgotten about the dogs. They would have sprung upon him and torn him to pieces. But two servants grabbed them by the collar and held them back, snarling and yelping and gnashing their teeth, while he unbolted the door and flung it open. Danae was sitting on her stool in the darkness. In her arms was a baby, and his face shone like the morning star.

Acrisius would have killed them on the spot, and it was not his daughter's beauty or pity for the child which held him back. He dared not do it. Instead he called for his guards to drag them to the seashore. There he threw them into a wooden chest and, banging down the lid, kicked it out into the waves. And

the wind and current caught the chest and swept it far out into the Aegean sea.

It was midwinter and the sea was rough. The chest was as dark as the underground prison had been, but colder and more cramped and much noisier. Inside, Danae felt as if she had been tied up in the bag of the winds or trapped in the halls of thunder. When the waves struck the chest, she was hurled against the

sides and bruised, and the water oozed through the
hinges and cracks and soaked her. She clasped the baby
tightly in her arms. Whenever the waves were quiet,
she sang to him softly and he slept without waking,
his face radiant in the gloom. When the thunder of
the sea made her heart sink with terror, still he slept
serenely on and gave her courage. During the night a
wave smashed the bronze lock and the lid flew open,

nearly spilling them into the sea. Then she lay in the bottom of the chest and clung on and at last fell asleep, exhausted.

In the morning the wind had dropped and the sea was calm. She looked out and saw a nest floating on the water with two kingfishers in it. These were Halcyone and her lover, who had once been mortal; when one of them had drowned, to save them from despair the gods had changed them into kingfishers. And now each winter for seven clear days the winds are quiet and the kingfisher and her mate sit brooding on their nest as it floats on the quiet sea. As Danae watched, her terror melted. The halcyon days had come and she had no more to fear from wind or waves.

All day long the chest drifted with the current. At night the stars came out and shone brightly over the winter sea. Then Danae, clasping the baby to her, looked up at the highest and brightest of them and prayed:

> *Hesperus, evening star,*
> > *Who guided the sun to the west,*
> *The shepherd's flock to the fold,*
> > *The child to his mother's breast,*
> *Bring us to welcoming shores*
> > *Where we may rest.*

2

DICTYS THE FISHERMAN

NEXT morning, on the shore of the island of Seriphos some fishermen were walking to their work. They carried tridents in their hands for spearing fish, and Dictys their leader had a casting net over his shoulder.

'That's a strange fish over there,' said Dictys, pointing to a dark shape bobbing up and down in the water. 'What is it—a shark, or a whale?'

They climbed over the rocks to get a closer look, but the shape came no nearer. So Dictys threw his net and caught it in the meshes and hauled it to his feet. It was a wooden chest. Danae had closed the lid before dawn to keep out the cold, and it had jammed. But they soon prised it open with their tridents and found her and Perseus inside.

'This is a curious gift for the god Poseidon to send us,' said Dictys. 'Who are you, lady, and where do you come from?'

Danae clutched the sleeping baby to her and would not answer.

But Dictys only laughed. 'Well, if you will not

tell me your name, I must begin by telling you mine.
I am Dictys, the man of nets. Will you step ashore?'
And he held out his hand.

Soaked and cramped as she was, Danae seemed in
no hurry to take it. So Dictys stepped into the water

and pushed the chest round into the shallows and
beached it on the sand. Danae could hardly stay in
the chest for ever, and when Dictys held out his hand
a second time she took it and stepped timidly on to
the sand.

'I am not as rough as I look,' said Dictys. 'I may be only a poor fisherman, but my brother is Polydectes, king of the island.'

Danae sat down on the sand, and the fishermen crowded round to look at the baby.

'He has opened his eyes,' said one.

'They are like pools of sunlight,' said another.

'He smiles like a god,' said Dictys.

'He is the son of immortal Zeus,' said the mother. 'And I am Danae, whom Zeus has loved.'

'The son of Zeus!' said Dictys. 'How is it that a wife and child of Zeus can be treated so cruelly and cast adrift like this? The chest would look well in a palace, but it is hardly fit for the sea.'

With many tears Danae told them all that had happened since her father had shut her in the underground prison. Then the fishermen knelt on the sand and bowed to them. They could not doubt that her story was true.

'My wife and I are no longer young and we have no children of our own,' said Dictys. 'You shall come and live with us. It will be an honour to have you.'

So Danae and Perseus were welcomed in the fisherman's cottage, and there they lived happily with Dictys and his wife.

3

THE PROMISE

DICTYS brought the boy up as if he were his own son. He taught him to run and wrestle, to throw the quoit and the javelin, to fish and sail and swim; he taught him to protect his mother, to be brave and self-reliant. From Danae he learnt to be courteous and kind and to trust the gods, especially the goddess Athene. It was Athene who looked after women's crafts—the spinning and weaving and woolwork which Danae loved. It was she who guided the steps of the heroes, and Danae wanted Perseus to become one of them. So the boy began to serve in Athene's temple. By the time he reached manhood there was no one braver, more clever and handsome than he. Polydectes the king was jealous of him and hated him. He had a good reason for wishing him out of the way—he had fallen in love with Danae and wanted to force her to marry him. He could not do that while Perseus was there to protect her. How could he get rid of him?

At last he thought of a plan. He announced that he

was going to marry a wealthy lady named Hippo-dameia, though he did not really intend to. Then he invited to the palace all the chief men of the island including Perseus. As a wedding present each guest, he said, was to bring a horse. He knew that fishermen do not breed horses and it was unlikely that anyone living in a humble cottage could afford to buy one. He hoped to shame Perseus into quitting the island and leaving his mother behind.

The day of the feast arrived. The guests assembled in the palace courtyard with their horses, splendid in harnesses of silver and gold, and the air rang gaily with wedding bells. One by one Polydectes received them. Perseus came last of all.

'Where is your gift, Perseus?' said Polydectes.

'Sir, I have brought none.'

'Many rival suitors have come all the way from Greece with their gifts. What chance have I against them if you come here empty-handed?'

'I have no horse and no money to buy one.'

'You have brought me nothing at all?'

'Only my youth and skill,' said Perseus. 'But if you really mean to marry this lady and not my mother, I will bring you any gift you like to ask for.' And with a flash of reckless courage he added, 'Even the Gorgon's head.'

'Then bring it,' said Polydectes very quickly, before Perseus could change his mind.

At once Perseus regretted his words, for he had promised the impossible. The Gorgons were three sisters who lived at the end of the world, beyond the Ocean, in the kingdom of Night. Their heads and bodies were twined about with snakes instead of hair. They had swine's tusks in their cheeks, bronze hands and bronze wings that thundered in the air when they flew. They turned to stone anyone who looked at them. Two of them were immortal like the gods, but the third and most terrible of them was mortal. Her name was Medusa, and it was her head that he had rashly offered to fetch.

4

THE GODDESS ATHENE

PERSEUS ran from the palace to the farthest end of the island and sat on the shore cursing himself for a fool. If only he had a ship of his own! But what ship would take him to the edge of the world and the kingdom of Night? And if he ever reached it, how would he find the Gorgons? Yet somehow he must find the way. If he did not keep his word, he would have to leave the island in shame and his mother would be at the mercy of Polydectes.

Then in his trouble he remembered Athene, the goddess whom he served. He ran back over the hills to her temple, and had hardly begun his prayer when she appeared from behind the altar and stood at his side. Her wings were swan-white and her eyes as green as the sea. She had a golden helmet, a javelin and a shield, and she wore a long gown with a figured border.

'Perseus, I heard your prayer,' she said. 'You have served me since you were a child. Tell me how I can help you.'

Perseus fell on his knees and told her of the promise he had made to Polydectes.

'You spoke rashly,' said Athene.

Perseus bowed his head.

'But bravely too,' she added. 'I know the Gorgon Medusa. She was once a maiden with cheeks like spring blossom. But she sinned against the gods and I punished her. I made tusks sprout from her cheeks, I changed her locks to hissing snakes. She is my enemy. If you destroy her, you will serve my purpose and your own. Cut off her head and bring it to me.'

'How can I go near her?' said Perseus. 'She will turn me into stone.'

'I will give you my polished shield,' said Athene. 'Look at her reflection in the shield, not at her, and she cannot harm you.'

'She lives in the kingdom of Night. How can I hope to find her?'

'The gods will show you the way.'

'I have no ship.'

'A ship would be useless. Be patient and the gods will give you all you need for the journey.'

She waved her javelin and the bronze doors of the temple swung open, flooding it with light. There was a white cloud in the sky and out of it leapt winged

Hermes, the messenger of the gods. He ran down the long lane of sunlight and stood at Perseus's feet.

'I bring you my winged sandals,' he said. 'They will carry you over the sea and over the mountains, swifter than any swallow. They will not let your feet wander from the way.'

He knelt down and fastened them to the young man's ankles. Before Perseus could thank him he had vanished. But the great doors still stood open and the brightness outside seemed to beckon Perseus. Athene took him by the hand and led him out of the temple into the sun.

'There are three more things you will need for your journey,' she said. 'The fountain nymphs have them, and they live in a cave on the northern shore of the island. I will take you there.'

Perseus ran towards the road that led to the northern shore, eager to set off. But Athene called him back.

'Have you forgotten your wings already?' she said. 'This is the way you should go.' And she pointed to the white cloud from which Hermes had appeared.

Perseus sprang into the air. There was a fluttering of feathers about his ankles and he ran up the lane of light towards the sun. Then Athene leapt, lashing the air with her strong wings. She soon caught him up,

and together they sped through the white cloud. They came down among the mountains of the northern shore, sweeping down in great spirals like two eagles seeking their nest among the crags. Close to where their feet touched the rock a fountain bubbled from the ground and flowed down the mountain towards

the sea. Behind them was a steep cliff, and in the cliff
a cave.

'The nymphs of the fountain live here,' said Athene.
'They serve the gods and the heroes and will give you
all you need for your journey. Here they come.'

Out of the darkness of the cave the three nymphs

stepped. They wore long gowns and their hair was garlanded with flowers. Each offered a gift to Perseus.

'I bring you the cap of darkness,' said the first nymph. 'It is given you by the Lord of the Underworld. I have been deep down into the earth to fetch it. Wear it when you come to the Gorgons, and it will make you invisible.'

'I bring you a sword to strike off the Gorgon's head,' said the second nymph. 'It looks like a reaping hook, but the blade has an edge of diamonds that will cut through bronze. You will not need to strike twice.'

'I bring you a bag for her head,' said the third nymph. 'As soon as you have cut it off, put it inside and you will be safe.'

Perseus accepted the gifts gratefully. Then the three nymphs sat down by the fountain and drank, for they received life from its waters. They were neither mortal like men nor immortal like the gods, but so long as the fountain was there for them to drink, death could not touch them. When they had satisfied their thirst, they filled a cup and brought it to Perseus to drink. Then, happy and refreshed, he said goodbye to them and they went back to their cave.

'I will give you my shield now,' said Athene. 'Remember to use it as I told you.'

Perseus thanked her and put his left arm through the leather straps. He now had all he needed for his journey, and he asked her which way he should go.

'Fly northwards to the farthest edges of the world, to the kingdom of Night. The lights of heaven vanish there and are kindled again, for it borders on east and west. After their day's journey through the sky, the tired horses of the sun rest there until morning. It is there in the heart of darkness that the Gorgons live.'

'How shall I find them?'

'Go to their sisters, the three grey daughters of the Greybeard of the sea. They will tell you where the Gorgons live. Now, Perseus, it is time for you to go.'

He asked if he might say good-bye to his mother, but Athene would not let him. She was afraid that Danae's tears might distress him and sway him from his purpose. 'Dictys will look after her. I will comfort her for you,' she said.

Then Perseus sprang into the air and was gone.

5

THE THREE GREY SISTERS

HE ran along the sky, he cut through the cloud. He flew over the mountains and the valleys as far as his wings would carry him, to the far side of Ocean, where the kingdom of Night begins. Everything was grey here—the fields and thorn forests were grey, and so were the cliffs and the sky. There were no paths of any kind, for no man had ever been there before.

Perseus landed at the water's edge and walked over the rocks till he came to a cave. And there in the grey twilight he saw the three Grey Sisters with their grey cheeks and their long grey hair, sitting in silence by the sluggish sea. They kept watch turn about, for they had only one eye and one tooth between them. And they were so still they might have been carved of rock.

He called to them suddenly and fiercely, 'Grey Sisters, where do the Gorgons live?'

They had not heard a human voice before. They shuddered and trembled like shadows in a pool ruffled by the wind. They fumbled with the eye and passed it from hand to hand as each in turn fitted it

into her forehead. But they could not see him, for he was wearing the cap of darkness.

'Daughters of the Greybeard of the sea, where do the Gorgons live?'

'We shall not tell you,' they answered. 'Who are you and who sent you here?'

'I am Perseus, one of the sons of men. Athene sent me.'

'Athene is our enemy,' cried one of them. 'We would not tell you even if you were the son of Zeus himself.'

'There must be some path through the forests.'

'There is none!' they cried.

'Then I will fly over the mountains.'

'The cold would kill you.'

'Do they live beyond the mountains?'

'No.'

'Then where are they hiding?'

The Grey Sisters would not answer.

There was a long silence. Perseus watched them carefully, but they did not move, except for the smallest Sister. She wore the eye and was turning her head from side to side, peering into the twilight.

Then Perseus said, 'Grey Sisters, shall I tell you where *I* am hiding?'

'Tell us, Perseus, tell us!' they cried with one voice.

'Where only the tallest of you could see me,' said Perseus. 'Give her the eye.'

The smallest removed it from her forehead and the tallest reached out with her skinny hand. But she never received it, for, while it was passing, Perseus slipped his fingers into the grey palm and snatched it. Then he sprang into the air. Hovering over their heads, he cried out, 'Tell me the way to the Gorgons. If not, I shall throw your eye into the sea and you will be blind for ever.'

Then he swooped in the air above them and made such a fluttering about their ears that in panic they cried out the answer, 'Through the cave!'

They reached up with their skinny hands to catch him, but he sprang up out of their reach and all they caught was one small feather from his wings.

'We have told you our secret—now give us back our eye!' they cried.

'You shall have it,' said Perseus. 'But I warn you, if you have lied to me I shall soon be back to take my revenge.'

He tossed the eye to them. Luminous in the twilight, it slithered over the rocks into the grey sand at their feet. And they fell on their knees and scratched for it, wailing and lamenting all the time.

Perseus did not wait. He passed into the cave.

6

THE GORGON'S HEAD

THE lamentations of the Grey Sisters followed him, growing weaker and weaker the farther he flew. The cave was very dark, but the rocks below him were furred with phosphorus and he followed their green trail far into the darkness.

Soon the air began to hum with the whirr of tiny wings. At first he thought he had disturbed the spirits of the cave, until he looked up and saw that they were bats. They swooped down upon him from the roof. They ruffled his hair, they skimmed past his cheek, but they never touched him.

On and on he flew, till far in front of him he saw a faint light. It grew bigger as he came near, and the whirr of wings died away. Then there was no darkness at all, only grey twilight and a wilderness of rocks. He had passed under the mountain and come out on the other side. Many of the rocks were shaped like beasts and monsters, which one look at Medusa's face had turned to stone. He knew now that the Gorgons could not be far away.

Suddenly, as he wheeled past a cliff, he came upon them. They were asleep in a nest among the rocks, their cheeks pillowed on their brass hands, their golden wings folded round them. And they were snoring like pigs. Careful not to look directly at Medusa, he stared at her reflection in Athene's shield. He could see the boar's tusks that sprouted from her cheeks, and the snakes that girdled her body and coiled about her face—they too were asleep. Then he alighted softly on the rocks beside her and drew his sword. The snakes were waking now, they began to writhe and hiss. And Medusa sighed as she slept. She stirred and grunted; her heavy eyelids quivered as they opened. But Perseus was too quick for her. Still looking at her reflection in the bronze shield, he raised the sword and—while Athene guided his hand—struck hard. With one blow he cut the head from the neck. He caught it by the snaky locks, thrust it into the bag and sprang into the air.

Then a strange thing happened. As the body fell back and the brass wings clattered on the rocks, a beautiful white creature leapt from the pool of Medusa's blood. It was the winged horse Pegasus. He lashed the air with his wings, he thrashed with his powerful hoofs, and away he flew over half the world to Mount Helicon where the Muses live.

Perseus did not wait, for already the other two Gorgons, the immortal ones, were moving. The clatter of Medusa's body as she fell had roused them. When they saw her lying there, they howled; they rattled their brass wings and sprang into the air after Perseus. They could not see him, for he was wearing the cap of darkness and was away hot haste along the pathways of the air; but as they sniffed about them

they caught the scent of Medusa's blood. Their
heavy wings were no match for the winged sandals.
On and on Perseus flew, with the sword at his side,
the bag slung from his shoulder and Medusa's head
safe inside it. The Gorgons dropped far behind and
their howling became fainter and fainter. And Perseus passed beyond the kingdom of Night and saw
them no more.

But he was not out of danger yet. Stormy winds drove him round the world, north to the freezing stars, then south to the equator, then east, then west, then back again. At last, as daylight was fading, he reached the borders of the west, the kingdom of the giant Atlas. It was nearly dark and he was too exhausted to go on. So he decided to come down and rest here till morning.

7

THE GIANT ATLAS

ATLAS was the biggest giant alive. He ruled over the edge of the world, where the horses of the sun plunged into the sea after their day's journey. He had a thousand flocks of sheep and a thousand herds of cattle wandering on the plains, also an orchard with a tree whose leaves and fruit and branches were all of shining gold. It was surrounded by a high wall and guarded by a dragon, who prowled round it to keep off strangers.

Perseus flew above the orchard out of reach of the dragon and landed at the giant's feet.

'Sir, I beg you to let me rest here tonight,' he said.

Atlas stared down at him and said not a word.

'I have flown over half the world and my deeds are famous,' said Perseus. 'If you honour great deeds, you will surely welcome me here.'

As the giant considered what Perseus said, the fires of the sunset glowed in his eyes. But still he said nothing.

'Does high birth mean anything to you?' said

Perseus. 'Do you know that I am the son of Zeus, the King of Heaven?'

At the name of Zeus, Atlas started. An old prophet had once told him that the time would come when his tree would be stripped of its gold, and the thief would be the son of Zeus. That is why he had built the wall round the orchard and set the dragon to keep guard.

'Go away from here! You are a braggart and a liar,' he thundered, and the earth shook with his anger.

'Sir, I swear I have told you the truth.'

'Go away!'

But Perseus stood his ground.

Reaching forward, Atlas struck him with the palm of his hand and knocked him over. Perseus sprang up again.

'What have I done to deserve this?' he said.

'You have come to steal my golden apples.'

'I would not dream of touching them, except as a gift.'

'You shall have no gifts from me!'

Perseus tried to calm the giant and reason with him, but Atlas answered him only with force. He reached down towards Perseus with his huge hairy arms, meaning to throw him into the sea. But Perseus caught him round his right knee and clung on. He

tried to draw his sword, but Atlas plucked him off and wrestled with him. For all his courage, Perseus was no match for such crude strength, and soon he lay sprawling on the ground with the giant's foot across his chest. With a great effort he wriggled free.

'I did not start this quarrel with you,' he gasped, struggling to his feet.

Atlas kicked him down again and would have crushed him with his foot, but Perseus was too nimble. Turning away his head, he slipped his hand into the bag and took out the Gorgon's head.

'I asked very little of you and you refused it,' he said. 'Now I will leave you a gift that you will not forget.' And he held up the terrible head, its face towards the giant.

At once Atlas became a mountain. His beard and hair were changed to forests, his arms and shoulders to long ridges. His head was the summit, his bones were rocks and stones. Then he swelled to monstrous size, till he filled the whole space between earth and sky. And there he stood, his tremendous shadow stretched across the land, and heaven and all the stars heaped on his shoulders.

Tired out, Perseus lay down in the giant's palace and slept.

He woke a little before dawn to see the horses of

the sun splashing in the sea. After his night's rest he felt as fresh as they, glad too that the day was calm and still, for Aeolus, lord of the winds, had shut them in their prison.

It was time for the horses to start their day's journey, and he watched them climb into the sky with their chariot of fire. Higher and higher they climbed, till he could no longer see them at all, only the blazing disc of the sun bringing light and warmth to the world.

Then he put on his winged sandals, picked up his sword and shield, and slung the bag over his shoulder. He leapt up and ran along the pathways of the air, away from the kingdom of Night and back to the lands of men.

8

THE PRINCESS CHAINED TO
THE ROCKS

OVER vast stretches of sea he flew, over wild mountains and lonely sun-scorched deserts where nothing grew. As he went, blood-drops from the Gorgon's head fell down to the sand, where they turned into poisonous snakes, which breed there to this day.

Then the wind blew on the sand and whirled it into the sky, blotting out the sun and the land so that he could not see where he was going. There was sand in his hair, sand in his eyes, sand in his clothing, sand in the bag with the Gorgon's head. It weighed him down and he cried out to the gods for help.

And suddenly Hermes was beside him, his hand on the leather strap, helping him to bear the weight.

'Do not lose heart, Perseus,' he said. 'There is still more for you to do, more fame to win. Close your eyes, bend your head into the storm, and strive with all your might.'

Perseus obeyed, and the strength of the gods flowed into his limbs and gave him power to fight the storm. When he opened his eyes again, he was alone in the sky. Hermes had vanished, the sun was shining and there was no wind at all.

At last he came to Ethiopia. Floating down the air he saw the coast far below him, with dark cliffs and a crawling sea. And suddenly, as he rounded a headland, he saw a body on the rocks. It was a girl, with her arms chained to the cliff and the waves snarling at her feet. She leaned there so white and still that she might have been a statue. Only her hair stirring in the breeze and the warm tears that trickled down her cheeks showed that she was alive. And she was so beautiful that Perseus almost forgot to move his wings.

He alighted near her and went slowly towards her.

'Who are you, and why are you chained here?' he asked.

She was too shy to answer and would have hidden

her face in her hands, but they were bound. Only her eyes were free and they filled with tears and sparkled like the jewelled necklace at her throat.

'You need not be afraid of me,' said Perseus. 'I am a Greek and will help you if I can.'

'My name is Andromeda,' she answered, reassured by his gentle words. 'My father is Cepheus, king of this land, and my mother is Queen Cassiope.'

'But why should a princess be in chains?'

'My mother boasted that I was more beautiful than the Nereids, the goddesses of the sea. Poseidon, king of the sea, was jealous and flooded our cities. He sent a monster from the deep to devour us and—'

'Has Cepheus not tried to slay the monster?'

'He cannot. The oracle has told him *I* must be slain. I am to be sacrificed to the monster. That is why I am waiting here in chains.'

'And your father has left you here to die?'

'The people forced him to. He had no choice.'

'Is there nobody brave enough to save you?' asked Perseus. 'Have you no champion, no friend?'

'I am engaged to my uncle Phineus.'

'He should be here to defend you. Where is he?'

'Hiding in his palace, I expect,' said Andromeda bitterly.

Perseus was so angry that he could not speak. He tore at the chains and tried to wrench them from the rock, but they were too strong for him. He looked wildly round for help. A great crowd had gathered on the beach, wailing and lamenting. At their head were the King and Queen.

'What is the use of tears?' said Perseus, and he turned to the crowd. 'The Princess needs your help before it is too late. Go and fetch crowbars and files to break the chains.'

Nobody stirred.

Perseus ran lightly from rock to rock till he stood at the King's feet.

'I can do nothing,' said Cepheus—he did not dare to look him in the face. 'The oracle has decreed—'

'Andromeda is your daughter. Surely she means more to you than an oracle?' said Perseus. 'If you will not help her, then I will.'

'And who are you?' said Cepheus scornfully.

'My name is Perseus. I am the son of Zeus and Danae.'

'And you think yourself a match for this monster that has killed a hundred warriors and ravaged half our land?'

'I have slain the Gorgon,' said Perseus. 'Is that not proof enough for you? I would like to serve you, sir, and your daughter too. I will fight the monster and do my best to save her, for I love her with all my heart. But if I succeed, you must promise to let me marry her.'

'Impossible,' said Cepheus. 'She is engaged to Phineus.'

'Phineus is a coward. He is not worthy of her,' said Perseus. 'I have proved my courage and am ready to prove it again. She shall come home with me and be queen of Argos.'

At that moment Andromeda cried out in terror, for there on the rim of the sea was the dark shape of the monster.

9

THE SEA MONSTER

WITH a loud roar the monster came speeding towards the shore. It cut through the waves like a ship when the wind creaks in the rigging and the oarsmen sweat and strain.

The Queen threw herself at Perseus's feet and begged him to save her. 'You shall have her as your wife,' she said.

'And a kingdom for her wedding gift,' said Cepheus.

'Don't forget your promise,' said Perseus, and he drew his sword and stood waiting.

But the people scattered. They hid among the rocks and in the fields behind the cliffs.

On came the monster, dipping and plunging. Its back was scaly with barnacles that glistened in the sun; waves gushed in waterfalls from its jaw.

When it was a stone's throw from the cliff, Perseus sprang into the air. The monster could not see him. But it saw the hero's shadow on the water and furiously attacked it. Perseus could not help laughing, for the monster was snorting and puffing and lashing about with its wings, doing no damage to anything except its own temper. He raised his sword, ready to strike. Then he swooped down and buried it up to the hilt in its shoulder. Bellowing with pain the monster reared into the air, then plunged into the water. Like a wild boar chased by a pack of hounds, it dodged and twisted among the waves, snapping its cruel fangs. Thanks to his wings Perseus managed to escape. He kept darting in with his sword, jabbing it into the monster's back and sides and the base of its tail. Gradually it grew weaker, but Perseus's wings were soaked with spray and once its jaws nearly closed on his ankles. Just in time he grabbed at a rock and clung on to it with one hand. With the other he thrust the sword three times into the monster's heart. And the monster sank, never to rise again.

As Perseus fell back on to the rock, panting for breath, he heard a great shout behind him. The shore and the cliff-top were crowded with cheering people. They looked as if they had been there all the time and had never run away.

He flew to Andromeda, skimming over the tops of the waves. A smith had freed her from her chains and she ran forward to greet Perseus. He kissed her hand and asked her to be his bride.

'Take me as your servant, your slave; do what you will with me.'

'You shall be my queen—queen of Argos. Will you go there with me?'

'I would go with you to the ends of the earth,' she said.

Her parents were more grudging in their welcome. Now that their daughter was safe, they wanted to get rid of the young man. But Perseus held them to their promise and asked them to prepare the wedding feast at once.

'Your daughter wants to marry me. You heard

her say so,' he said. 'I am not taking her against her will. Remember, you promised me a kingdom too. But I do not mean to claim it. Andromeda is all I ask.'

Then servants brought him jugs of water and he washed his hands and body of all trace of the monster's blood. They took his sword and laid it down beside him. They tried to take the bag with the Gorgon's head as well, but he would not let them touch it. Telling them to stand back, he lifted it out. Then he carefully laid it face downwards upon a bed of leaves so as not to bruise it. At once the Gorgon's power passed into the leaves; they grew hard and stiff, like coral. The sea-nymphs were pleased with this and brought more leaves, and the same thing happened again. They were delighted with the stiff leaves and took them down to the sea. Coral is still like this today; under water it bends like a twig, but it hardens when exposed to the air.

As soon as he had washed and put on clean clothes, Perseus built three altars, one for each of the gods who had helped him. To Hermes he sacrificed a young bullock, to Athene a cow, and to Zeus a bull. Then he put back the Gorgon's head in the bag and set off for the palace.

10

THE FIGHT AT THE WEDDING FEAST

In the palace of King Cepheus the wedding feast was ready. The fires were heaped with incense; garlands were hung on the walls, and the roof rang to the sound of lyre and flute and harp. A great crowd of nobles and courtiers had gathered to see Perseus claim his bride.

Suddenly the golden doors opened and she came in, dressed in a long purple robe, with bracelets of gold and a necklace of a hundred blossoms. Her brides-maids came with her, each wearing a garland of violets. And as they led her to Perseus, they sang her wedding song:

> *Sweet maiden,*
> *Rose-red apple from the branch*
> *Nearest the sky,*
> *Poised beyond human grasp*
> *Where the swallows fly;*
> *Only the hero Perseus*
> *Could reach so high.*

After the ceremony came the feast, with more music and rejoicing. When all the guests had eaten and drunk their fill, Cepheus asked Perseus to tell them the story of his adventures, and they gathered round to listen.

He had hardly begun when the doors of the banquet hall flew open and a man, followed by a crowd of soldiers, burst in. He was bearded and broad-shouldered, and he held a spear of ashwood. It was Phineus, the King's brother.

'Where is Perseus?' he cried, leaping on to a table and kicking the wine bowls aside. Then he saw him sitting on a bench, with his arm round Andromeda's waist. 'You have stolen my bride,' he shouted. 'I have come for my revenge. Your wings will not save you this time.'

He poised his spear, took aim and hurled. But he was so angry that his hand was unsteady. The bronze point struck the bench and lodged there, the long shaft shivering. Perseus wrenched it out and was about to hurl it back, when Cepheus caught his arm.

'Brother, are you mad?' cried Cepheus, addressing Phineus, who had run and hidden behind the altar. 'Perseus is our honoured guest. He saved my daughter from the monster. Is this the way to thank him?'

'He stole my bride,' said Phineus.

'You abandoned her, you left her chained to the rock,' said Perseus. 'If she is so precious to you, why did you not try to save her? I have a better right to her than you.'

Meanwhile, more and more of Phineus's men were rushing into the hall. Cepheus seemed in no hurry to stop them, and he gave no orders to close the doors. This made Perseus suspicious. He turned and looked at Cepheus—who was just about to plunge a dagger in his ribs.

'Traitor!' cried Perseus. 'So you are both against me, and Phineus came at your command!'

He would have hurled his spear at him, but it was not safe to do so. Cepheus had taken Andromeda by the hand and was hurrying her to the back of the hall.

'Perseus forced this marriage upon us—it was not our wish,' he shouted. 'He must die!'

Then the whole mob went mad and hurled their spears. A few took Perseus's side and shouted that Cepheus should die as well as Phineus. But Cepheus was behind the pillars crying out to the gods, and Phineus was still hiding behind the altar.

Perseus snatched a log that lay smouldering on the altar and struck at anyone who dared to come near him. At his side was an old man with a grizzled white beard; he fought bravely till an arrow pierced his throat and he fell dead on the altar. Another arrow, aimed at Perseus, stuck in the folds of his robe. He was trying to find the man who shot it when a Syrian champion attacked him with a battle-axe. Perseus leapt on to the bench. Seizing a heavy mixing bowl and lifting it high up with both hands, he brought it crashing down on the Syrian's head.

When Phineus saw this, he was more frightened than ever. Only when Perseus's back was turned did he dare show himself. With trembling hand he hurled his javelin at him, but it missed and hit an Indian youth instead. The youth had wanted to keep out of the fight.

'Since you force me to take sides, I shall return this to you!' he cried, but he was weak from the wound and, when he tried to pull the javelin out of his body, he fainted.

Spears were flying thicker than hail. The floor was slippery with spilt wine, and the cries of the wounded echoed through the hall.

Perseus stood with his back against a pillar, fighting like a tiger. But more and more of Phineus's men kept pouring into the hall and he was no match for such numbers.

'You have forced me to it—you leave me no choice!' cried Perseus, thrusting his hand into the bag.

'Those who are my friends here, turn away your faces!' And he took out the Gorgon's head and lifted it on high.

'Try that magic on someone else—it doesn't frighten me!' said one of the soldiers.

He was just about to throw his javelin at Perseus when his right hand stiffened and he turned into stone. The same thing happened to another soldier who was lungeing at Perseus with his sword. The point was only a finger's breadth from his heart.

A braggart named Nileus came swaggering up. The seven mouths of the Nile were engraved on his shield, for he liked to claim that the river was his father.

'Perseus, you have no power over me,' he said. 'I shall kill—'

He never finished the sentence. As he turned into stone, his lips froze, half open.

Nileus had a companion named Eryx, who could not believe what he had just seen. He thought his friend had lost his nerve.

'What a coward you are, Nileus!' he cried. 'Rush in with me now and hurl this fellow to the ground.'

He began to charge, but his feet were rooted to the floor; there he stood, a statue in full armour.

All these deserved their fate. But one poor soldier, fighting bravely for Perseus, looked at the Gorgon by mistake. No one realized what had happened until a sword struck his arm with a clang, like the sound of a blow on the anvil. At the same moment the swordsman himself was turned to stone, with a look of amazement on his face.

Altogether two hundred men were turned into

stone. Another two hundred, of whom Phineus was
one, survived.

Phineus began to feel sorry now for what he had
done. His friends were all round him and he went up
to each in turn, calling them by name, but as he
touched them he felt the chill of stone. Then he knelt
before Perseus. Stretching out his hands in surrender,
he looked to one side and said, 'Take away the

Gorgon's head, take it away, I beg you. I never hated you. I was fighting for Andromeda because I loved her.'

'Your love is unworthy of her,' said Perseus.

'I claimed her before you did,' said Phineus.

'And now you ask me to give her back?'

'No, Perseus. All I ask is my life.'

'You are a coward, and I despise cowards,' said Perseus. 'But I will not kill you with my sword. I will make you into a monument. Your story will not be forgotten, for you will stand here in my father-in-law's house for ever.'

He stepped aside and held the Gorgon's head in front of Phineus, so that he could not help facing it. At once he was turned to stone; his pleading hands and cringing looks and even the tears on his cheeks were fixed in marble for ever.

11

THE RETURN HOME

So Perseus triumphed over his enemies and won for himself a beautiful princess. His happiness was complete.

But he had not forgotten his mother and he was anxious to know what had been happening to her all this time. Taking Andromeda by the hand, he flew with her over the sea back to the island of Seriphos.

They landed on the green cliff and ran through the fields to the village where his home was.

'It is no palace, only a poor fisherman's cottage,' said Perseus, and he told her how years ago he and his mother had come to live there with Dictys.

But when they turned by the harbour wall they saw no cottage but a ruin of tumbled stones and charred wood. And where were Dictys's boats? In the harbour below only the masts showed above the water—they had been holed and sunk.

Some children were playing among the crumbling walls.

'Have you seen my mother? Have you seen Dictys?'
said Perseus.

They gave only confused answers, and when he
asked about Polydectes they were afraid and ran away.

Then he remembered the goddess Athene who had
never failed him in his need, and they hastened to her
temple to ask for help. Some palace guards were

lounging outside. The hot sunshine had made them sleepy and they let Perseus and his bride pass. It was cool and quiet inside the temple. Suddenly Perseus heard the sound of weeping. Someone was crouching by the altar. It was his mother, Danae, who had come here to escape Polydectes and his guards.

When she saw Perseus she cried out with joy, and

at once all her troubles vanished. She clung to him and would not let him go, and it was some time before Perseus could make her realize that the beautiful princess with him was his wife. Then she tenderly kissed Andromeda too, and all three rejoiced together.

'Where is Dictys?' said Perseus.

'In prison,' said Danae. 'Polydectes has threatened to kill him. But you have slain the Gorgon and can surely save Dictys.'

'I hope I shall be in time,' said Perseus. And he told Andromeda and Danae to stay in the temple until he came back.

'The guards may kill you, Perseus,' said Danae, and she clung to him again.

'They will not dare to touch me,' said Perseus, and he told her what was in his bag.

12

PERSEUS KEEPS HIS PROMISE

PERSEUS went straight to the palace. As he hurried up the steps to the banquet hall, he could hear shouting and the sounds of revelry where Polydectes and his guests were feasting. He knocked on the door, but the noise was so loud that no one heard him. He burst it open and ran in.

The tables had been cleared and Polydectes and his nobles were lying on couches, while the wine cup passed from hand to hand. They did not look up at Perseus but went on singing their drinking song:

> *A cup for the honey-sweet wine,*
> *A garland of flowers for the head!*
>   *Drink deep while we may,*
>   *For we're living today*
> *But tomorrow we dwell with the dead.*

Tomorrow? They would not last so long.

Perseus swept up to where Polydectes was lying, fingering the delicate stem of his golden wine cup.

'Sir, I have kept my promise,' said Perseus.

Polydectes peered up at him with bleary drunken eyes. 'Who are you?' he said.

'I am Perseus, and I have brought you the Gorgon's head as I said I would. It was no easy task.'

Polydectes knew him, but he did not believe his words. He was angry and defiant.

'You have not killed the Gorgon. I will have you whipped from the palace for your lies!' He hurled the

wine cup to the ground, and all the guests shouted insults at Perseus.

'I have told you the truth—and here is my proof!' cried Perseus. 'Those who are my friends here, turn away your faces!' Before Polydectes had time to call his guards he lifted the Gorgon's head from the bag and held it up.

Polydectes was struggling to get up, one foot was pressing the floor, when his blood hardened and he turned to stone. A few escaped, but all those who came under the Gorgon's power froze where they stood. And there they stayed among the wine cups and the tables, till the rafters rotted and the pillars crumbled and grass and wild flowers sprang up round their feet. The circle of stones that was once Polydectes and his guests can be seen in Seriphos to this day.

Perseus returned at once to the temple and told his wife and mother what he had done. While he was still speaking, Athene appeared from the altar. She was radiant and smiling.

'Perseus, I am proud of you,' she said. 'You have proved your manhood and triumphed over the powers of darkness. You have cared for Danae as a son should care for his mother. Above all, you have obeyed the gods—and you have brought me the Gorgon's head. Give it to me now, for you will need it no more. I will fix it on my shield for ever, to strike terror in the enemies of gods and men.'

She took it from the bag, and her shield as well, while Perseus bowed his head in gratitude and reverence.

'You will no longer need the sandals. It is time to return them to Hermes,' she said.

She waved her javelin and the bronze doors of the temple swung open, flooding the stone floor with light.

There was a white cloud in the sky and out of it leapt winged Hermes, the messenger of the gods. He ran down the long lane of sunlight and stood at Perseus's feet.

Perseus unbound his sandals and gave them to him, also the sword and the bag and the cap of darkness. Hermes promised to return these to the nymphs of the fountain. Then, before Perseus had time to thank him, the winged messenger vanished into the cloud.

Athene followed soon after. Wrapped in the cloud, she left the island and flew over the sea to Mount Helicon, the home of the Muses. She had heard that the winged horse Pegasus had flown there, that he had stamped his hoof on a rock and a fountain had gushed forth, and she wanted to see it.

Meanwhile Perseus released Dictys from prison and made him king of Seriphos in his brother's place.

13

THE STRANGER AT THE GAMES

BUT the story of Perseus is not quite ended yet. He still thought sometimes of his grandfather Acrisius, who had so cruelly wronged his mother and thrown her and her baby to the waves. Yet he tried not to judge him too harshly. Many years had passed since then, and in spite of everything he was ready now to forgive him and be reconciled.

So he built a galley and, taking Andromeda and Danae with him, set sail for Argos, where Acrisius was still king. On his way he stopped at Larissa, where the king of the country was holding funeral games in honour of his dead father. As a youth in Seriphos, Perseus had been a champion in every sport. Here was

a chance to match himself against other athletes. So, without saying who he was, he asked the King of Larissa if he might take part, and the King agreed.

There were to be contests in running, jumping, wrestling and throwing the javelin and the discus, and a crown was to be won for each event.

'If I can win these crowns,' thought Perseus, 'I will take them to my grandfather and lay them at his feet.'

All the people of the town swarmed into the stadium. The King and Queen sat on the royal dais, under a canopy which shielded them from the hot sun. Danae and Andromeda sat near them as honoured guests.

Among the crowd at the other end of the stadium was an old man, a stranger whom no one seemed to know, for he came from a foreign country. He was very frail and his face was lined with suffering. He looked as if he had come to the games to try to forget his troubles.

The games began. Perseus soon showed that in running, jumping, wrestling and throwing the javelin there was no one to approach him. If he could win the discus throw too, all five crowns would be his. No athlete had ever been known to win all five championships before.

Perseus was the last to throw. As he stooped to pick up the discus, all eyes were upon him. Everyone wondered who the young stranger could be. He was so proud and handsome; he had won his crowns so easily. Could he be one of the heroes, a son of the immortal gods?

Perseus gripped the discus. For a moment he held it poised at arm's length behind him, then swung round and hurled. Away through the air it went, and landed level with the farthest throw. His second throw landed six yards farther, an easy winner.

The people cheered wildly. 'We have never seen such a champion. Let him throw once again!'

Straining with all his might, Perseus hurled for the third and last time. A gust of wind caught the discus and sent it spinning beyond the boundaries of the stadium, over the heads of the crowd. The frail old stranger saw it coming and covered his head. It struck his foot, and he cried out with the pain and fainted away.

Perseus ran at once to the old man, leaping over the stone benches. He lifted him up and held him in his arms, but the shock of the blow was too much and

life was already fading from his cheeks. He gave a sigh of infinite sadness, and as he died he gasped one word—the name of Danae.

'Who is this man?' said Perseus with trembling lips, and his cheeks turned pale as a terrible thought struck him.

He ran to Danae and told her what had happened and how the old man had spoken her name as he died.

'Quickly, take me to him!' she said.

She did not dare name the fear that was in her mind and had lain sleeping there for twenty years. But as soon as she saw the old man she knew it was true. The dead man was her father, Acrisius.

So the prophecy of the priest of Delphi was fulfilled. 'Your daughter will bear a son and he will kill you,' Acrisius had been warned. The fear of this had haunted him ever since. When he had heard that Perseus was on his way to Argos, dreading attack he had fled from the city to Larissa. He little knew that his grandson was going there too. But no man on earth can defeat the plans of the gods.

Perseus and Danae were deeply distressed. They had long ago forgiven Acrisius and all they wished for was reconciliation. Had he been sorry for his cruelty? Had he longed to see his daughter again, and was it only fear of meeting Perseus that had prevented him?

Now they would never know. They rent their clothes and wept for him. They burnt his body on a funeral pyre, and sadly Perseus threw into the fire the five crowns that he had won. The priests did their best to comfort him. They told him that as he had killed his grandfather by accident he was not guilty of his death. But Perseus would not be comforted. Still mourning his loss, with his wife and mother he sailed away from Larissa.

He did not go to Argos, for he was ashamed to reign where his grandfather had been king. Instead he changed kingdoms with his great-uncle Proetus and became ruler of the neighbouring city of Tiryns. Later he founded the great kingdom of Mycenae. The princess whom he had rescued from the sea monster brought him great joy. She bore him several sons and a daughter, and his life became so happy that in time he forgot the sorrow of his grandfather's death. He lived to a great age, and when he died he was buried in a hero's tomb.

TITLES IN THE NEW WINDMILL SERIES

Chinua Achebe: *Things Fall Apart*
Louisa M. Alcott: *Little Women*
Elizabeth Allen: *Deitz and Denny*
Margery Allingham: *The Tiger in the Smoke*
Michael Anthony: *The Year in San Fernando*
Enid Bagnold: *National Velvet*
Stan Barstow: *Joby*
H. Mortimer Batten: *The Singing Forest*
Nina Bawden: *On the Run; The Witch's Daughter; A Handful of Thieves*
Phyllis Bentley: *The Adventures of Tom Leigh*
Paul Berna: *Flood Warning*
Pierre Boulle: *The Bridge on the River Kwai*
E. R. Braithwaite: *To Sir, With Love*
D. K. Broster: *The Flight of the Heron; The Gleam in the North; The Dark Mile*
F. Hodgson Burnett: *The Secret Garden*
Helen Bush: *Mary Anning's Treasures*
A. Calder-Marshall: *The Man from Devil's Island*
John Caldwell: *Desperate Voyage*
Albert Camus: *The Outsider*
Victor Canning: *The Runaways; Flight of the Grey Goose*
Erskine Childers: *The Riddle of the Sands*
John Christopher: *The Guardians*
Richard Church: *The Cave; Over the Bridge; The White Doe*
Colette: *My Mother's House*
Lettice Cooper: *The Twig of Cypress*
Alexander Cordell: *The Traitor Within*
Meindert deJong: *The Wheel on the School*
Peter Dickinson: *The Gift*
Eleanor Doorly: *The Radium Woman; The Microbe Man; The Insect Man*
Gerald Durrell: *Three Singles to Adventure; The Drunken Forest; Encounters with Animals*
Elizabeth Enright: *Thimble Summer; The Saturdays*
C. S. Forester: *The General*
Eve Garnett: *The Family from One End Street; Further Adventures of the Family from One End Street; Holiday at the Dew Drop Inn*
G. M. Glaskin: *A Waltz through the Hills*
Rumer Godden: *Black Narcissus*
Margery Godfrey: *South for Gold*
Angus Graham: *The Golden Grindstone*
Graham Greene: *The Third Man and The Fallen Idol*
Grey Owl: *Sajo and her Beaver People*
G. and W. Grossmith: *The Diary of a Nobody*
René Guillot: *Kpo the Leopard*
Esther Hautzig: *The Endless Steppe*
Jan De Hartog: *The Lost Sea*
Erik Haugaard: *The Little Fishes*
Bessie Head: *When Rain Clouds Gather*

John Hersey: *A Single Pebble*
Georgette Heyer: *Regency Buck*
Alfred Hitchcock: *Sinister Spies*
C. Walter Hodges: *The Overland Launch*
Geoffrey Household: *Rogue Male; A Rough Shoot; Prisoner of the Indies*
Fred Hoyle: *The Black Cloud*
Irene Hunt: *Across Five Aprils*
Henry James: *Washington Square*
Josephine Kamm: *Young Mother; Out of Step; Where Do We Go From Here?*
Erich Kästner: *Emil and the Detectives*
John Knowles: *A Separate Peace*
D. H. Lawrence: *Sea and Sardinia; The Fox* and *The Virgin and the Gipsy; Selected Tales*
Marghanita Laski: *Little Boy Lost*
Harper Lee: *To Kill a Mockingbird*
Laurie Lee: *As I Walked Out One Mid-Summer Morning*
Ursula Le Guin: *A Wizard of Earthsea; The Tombs of Atuan; The Farthest Shore*
Doris Lessing: *The Grass is Singing*
C. Day Lewis: *The Otterbury Incident*
Lorna Lewis: *Leonardo the Inventor*
Martin Lindsay: *The Epic of Captain Scott*
Kathleen Lines: *The House of the Nightmare*
Jack London: *The Call of the Wild; White Fang*
Carson McCullers: *The Member of the Wedding*
Lee McGiffen: *On the Trail to Sacramento*
Wolf Mankowitz: *A Kid for Two Farthings*
Olivia Manning: *The Play Room*
James Vance Marshall: *A River Ran Out of Eden*
J. P. Martin: *Uncle*
John Masefield: *Sard Harker; The Bird of Dawning; The Midnight Folk; The Box of Delights*
W. Somerset Maugham: *The Kite and Other Stories*
Guy de Maupassant: *Prisoners of War and Other Stories*
Laurence Meynell: *Builder and Dreamer*
Yvonne Mitchell: *Cathy Away*
Honoré Morrow: *The Splendid Journey*
Bill Naughton: *The Goalkeeper's Revenge*
E. Nesbit: *The Railway Children; The Story of the Treasure Seekers*
E. Neville: *It's Like this, Cat*
Wilfrid Noyce: *South Col*
O'Brien: *Mrs Frisby and the Rats of NIMH*
Scott O'Dell: *Island of the Blue Dolphins*
George Orwell: *Animal Farm*
Merja Otava: *Priska*
John Prebble: *The Buffalo Soldiers*
J. B. Priestley: *Saturn Over the Water*
Lobsang Rampa: *The Third Eye*